Endorsements
by multi-published authors

The Steeple Chase by Carrie Fancett Pagels is a heartwarming story that takes readers on a 19th century ride through 1810 Virginia. The characters are examples of the Virginians of their day, with one adventurous heroine – the brave and determined Martha Osborne. Martha disguises herself as a man in order to 'race to the steeple' in hopes of winning so she can to bring her young brother Johnny back to her. Who doesn't love a heroine willing to put everything on the line for another? The romance and plot twists, the fleshed out characters, horses and races, will truly satisfy readers.

Rita Gerlach, *Dusk to Dawn Inspirational Fiction*

The Steeplechase is a fast-paced, well-rounded love story rich in historical detail that enriches the plot, rather than overwhelms it. I cared about the characters, too: Martha's tender heart for little Johnny drew me in! Another satisfying offering from Carrie Fancett Pagels.

Susanne Dietze, *Inspirational romance with historical charm, timeless heart*

The Steeplechase

A Love's Sporting Chance Novella

By

Carrie Fancett Pagels

This book is a work of fiction. Names, characters, places, and incidents are the product of the author's imagination and are used fictitiously. Any resemblance to actual events, locales, or persons, living or dead, is coincidental.

Copyright 2016 Carrie Fancett Pagels

First Edition

February, 2016

ASIN-10
ISBN-13: 978-0-9971908-1-6

No part of this book may be copied or distributed without the author's consent.

Cover by Cynthia Hickey

Hearts Overcoming Press

Dedicated
to
Elizabeth Christine Barden Cornett
My Forever Friend
You started me on this journey.
This one's for you, Libbie!!!

Characters

Heroine Martha Jane Osborne, 27, born 1783
    Father, Professor Osborne, 54, born 1756
    Stepmother, Letitia Collier Osborne 35, born 1775
    Brother, Johnny Osborne, 6, born 1804
    Brother, Christopher Osborne, 21, born 1789
    Sister, Emily Osborne, 14, born 1796
    Osborne servants, Dicey and Jessamine
    Galileo, her brother's horse
    Graham Tarleton, 24, Christopher's "friend"

Phillip Lucien Paulson, 29, born 1780
    Brother, George Joseph Paulson, 33, born 1777
    Sister-in-law, Andrée Duplessis Paulson, 27
    Uncle Gabriel Lightfoot
    Miranda Lightfoot – his cousin
    Othello, his horse

Chapter 1

Yorktown, Virginia
Autumn 1810

After hoisting the last child down from his horse, Phillip Lucien Paulson swatted dirt from his buckskin riding trousers, more content than he'd been in most of his twenty-nine years. Perhaps there really was something positive in his brother's desire to leave management of his father's plantation to others and begin an academy for planters' sons, instead.

"Playing stableboy again?" The headmaster's wife, Andrée, sidled up next to him, her scathing tone sending his good mood into flight, joining the squawking geese in the cerulean skies overhead.

Andrée laughed as she strolled across the yard, her skirts swaying as she headed toward the new grand home Phillip's brother, her husband, had built for her. So now not only would Andrée and George inherit the Paulson estate further up the York River, but they had another grand home to enjoy until their father died. And meanwhile, they tolerated Phillip as best they could. Hard to believe beautiful young Andrée Duplessis once claimed to fancy him and allowed Phillip to court her — until she'd learned he was the younger son.

Laughter interrupted his thoughts. Nearby in the stable, the children began cleaning their tack, with Mr. Lacey assisting them. Phillip brushed down his horse and curried him.

Within the half hour, all the primary lads at Yorkview Academy ran off from their equestrian lesson, save one—a tiny fellow. Johnny's impish smile conjured up images of someone whose portrait Phillip had recently viewed, but not with the child's same surname. He shook off the associated memory. Weren't most wealthy Virginians all related to one another? Wasn't young Osborn's mother a Randolph? Who knew how many Randolph relations' portraits hung on the walls of the Virginia plantations he'd visited throughout his life.

Phillip brushed down the child's mount, a docile gray mare, one of his favorites from their own family stable at Paulson's.

"Sir?"

"Yes?" He continued grooming the horse. What was such a young boy doing here? Had Phillip's brother taken leave of his senses? George may enjoy playing the part of headmaster for now, but even he had enough sense to not accept a child unsuitable for boarding school.

"Sir, do you know how to read?" A lock of chestnut hair fell across the boy's wide brow.

Phillip set aside the stiff boar's bristle brush and switched to a currycomb. By the time Phillip was this lad's age, he'd been reading Homer. Too bad his intellect hadn't won him any favors with his older brother. "Indeed, I can, Johnny."

"Truly?" His dark eyes grew wide. "I prayed somebody had taught you, sir."

"Oh? You prayed, Johnny?" Few of the boys spoke of their faith, although his brother did instruct them in religion—or at least in George's legalistic version of Christianity.

"Yes, I 'spected you might be able to read, sir." His tiny mouth quirked to the right.

Phillip straightened, catching a whiff of leather, horsehair, and his own sweat. He'd made a habit of not disclosing that he was only a volunteer at the school, not an employee. Neither did he nor George divulge that Phillip—their equestrian instructor and occasional stable helper—was brother to the headmaster. That secret was one for the boys to figure out. "You'd be correct in your intuitions, because I'm not really a stableboy—but don't tell anyone. All right?"

Would simple workmen one day have the privilege of an education now only afforded to the wealthy? Rumors of public education systems were growing and were a welcome concept in this new, great, and independent country. Those in the western territories and the Ohio Valley espoused such sentiments. "Surely my brother and the teachers are instructing you in your letters, are they not?"

The boy poked his index finger at the corner of his mouth. "They do. No one reads to me, though."

A child of such tender age needed a parent to tell him stories, tuck his covers all around him, and put him to bed in his own home with his family nearby. "Come. Sit. I'll tell you a story." He pointed to a bale of hay.

"But it's not bedtime."

"Ah. As I suspected. You're missing your mother." He offered what he hoped was a gentle smile. Given Phillip's sharp features, such a feat was accomplished only with much difficulty.

"No. My sister—she reads to me every night." Johnny nodded for emphasis, eyes wide.

The mare stomped her foot impatiently, and Phillip whispered to her and resumed his currying. "You've been blessed with a good sister, then."

"The best." The child's lower lip quivered. "And she's got to be terrible lonesome without me there."

Phillip glanced over the animal's back. "I imagine so."

"And she always took my sheets off for me and changed them in the night." Johnny hung his head.

Phillip stiffened and patted the mare on the back. The boys at Academy were expected to be fully dry through the night and to not soil their bedclothes. "Are you having a problem here?"

"Jace Tyler helps me, but he says if I don't stop soon, I'll probably get a caning."

Not if Phillip had anything to say about it. He'd confront his brother and have the child returned home as soon as possible. He'd heard from Andrée that the mother insisted Johnny attend boarding school despite her husband being on staff at the College of William and Mary. And the mother and sister were off to England, the older brother at college. "Is there no one at your home, besides your father, who could care for you?"

The lad blinked at him several times. "I just told you, my sister. She's old—like you."

He laughed. When he was Johnny's age, he'd considered almost thirty to be old, too.

"She's twenty plus this many." He held up seven stubby fingers.

"Ah, well she's not quite as old as the codger I am." He winked at the boy and then mussed his hair. *Within months I'll be thirty and yet unmarried, although not from the want of trying.* Phillip cringed recalling Andrée's cutting words when she'd made it clear that George, not he, was her true pursuit.

One of the academy stable hands approached them. "Sorry I'm late, sir."

"No problem. All is well."

Johnny sucked in a big breath and whispered, "But, sir, we can't have a story if that man stays here."

What did Phillip have to rush home to? His stable was full of premium horses whose ranks continue to swell and were well-tended by his hands. His dogs, too, were fit as a fiddle. And his father spent more time in Washington City and visiting his plantation-owning friends than he did trying to manage Paulson Farms. This child needed him. "I'll stay and read to you later."

"Would you like to see my quilt and my soffy?"

"Your soffy?"

"Yes, he's a soffy bear."

"Ah. I imagine he's stuffed with sawdust and not a live bear, is he?" Phillip's lips twitched as he stifled a grin.

"No, sir. Headmaster wouldn't allow that!"

No, indeed, Headmaster would not. Why then, had he allowed a child so young to remain at school?

Morning dew cloaked Martha Jane Osborne's burgundy walking gown and cream pelisse in an ethereal mist as the Virginia sun rose over Williamsburg. Conflicted over the events of the past week, she almost didn't notice the young man lingering on the corner at Duke of Gloucester street. Being the daughter of Williamsburg's two biggest pariahs had its advantages—such as the freedom to note which gentlemen had the audacity to stare outright at her as she passed them. And although she should keep her eyes demurely cast down, she met Thaddeus's salacious gaze with a scowl. "Mr. Nelson?"

"You oughtn't be walking by yourself." The lout offered an arm covered in a jacket so tightly tailored that he scarce could move the appendage away from his body. Although the dandy may have thought the garment well displayed his physique, it only called attention to how impractical Thad was—had always been. Although the same might also be said of her.

Hadn't she, in fact, the evening before, instead of making a practical plan to solve her problems, instead prayed for God to send her an angel? She sighed.

Ignoring the proffered arm, Martha lifted her chin. "I'm capable of walking four blocks by myself and back, thank you very much. And why aren't you working at your father's warehouse?"

"Mind your own business," Thaddeus mumbled as he swiveled away from her, muttering something no doubt derogatory about women as he went.

She stifled a giggle. Although Thad was annoying, he was harmless—unlike some of the other dandies in Tidewater Virginia.

Ahead of her, servant girls walked toward the market area at the heart of the street. A bright red bandana covered the head of a girl not much older than Martha's sister, Emily. The Osborne's kitchen maid, a freewoman, would normally be the one completing Martha's errand. But with Letitia returned to England, and Father at the college teaching classes this morning, Martha was free to do as she wished. Such had been the case every time Letitia crossed the ocean to her homeland. At seven and twenty, Martha had been in charge of the household for over four of the last ten years. She sighed. If only her stepmother understood how their neighbors looked down their noses at them because of those many long trips to England—a country they were only too happy to be free from.

She sighed. Perhaps things would change. Hadn't she begged God to bring her help? She needed her little brother brought home again, and not cloistered off in a school. Martha required a place of her own, for when Letitia returned. Allowing the woman's cutting words to continue to abrade her spirit would be like leaving a handful of chestnut burrs under Galileo's saddle and continuing to ride him.

A slight breeze swirled leaves around her pumps as Martha stopped to tug at the strings of her leather pouch. She peered inside and recounted her coins before continuing on.

"Mornin', Miss." The street sweeper dipped his head as she passed.

Martha pressed her lips together. She didn't wish to be unkind, but a social exchange between the two of them truly was untoward—as her refined stepmother reminded her at every opportunity. Was that how her fellow Virginians saw her Anglican father and her British mother—two people with whom a social exchange would be perceived as inappropriate? Didn't residents' frozen countenances and pursed lips announce as much? She'd not be so cold as they were.

"Good day, Mr..." Hadn't someone called him by an Old Testament name? "Hezekiah."

Warm brown eyes, surrounded by a mass of wrinkles, met hers and widened. Grizzled hair peaked from beneath his gray knit work cap. "Bless you, Miss. Mornin' to you, also."

Her cheeks warmed as she offered the man a fledgling smile before she continued up the street to the bakers. There, she'd done it! She'd defied the very conventions which held her family in a perpetual state of limbo. Her father's family members were not British aristocrats like her step-grandparents, nor were they simply college town Americans. Surely God knew what her place was. How she yearned for a country home where she could ride Galileo to her heart's content and not worry about what any neighbors might say. Instead, she had to sneak out like a thief to relish her one joy in life—besides spending time reading to her brother, who was now sent off to boarding school. She closed her eyes tightly, willing back any recalcitrant tears, and walked on toward the market.

Smoke spiraled up from the many establishments that crowded the long thoroughfare. Sweet yeasty scents drew her closer to her destination. Her stomach rumbled at the reminder that she'd partaken of nothing that morning other than a tepid cup of tea. Martha pulled her full skirt as she opened the door to the place where all her baked goods would be obtained for at least the following month while Stepmother was gone.

"Good day." Myrtle James cocked her head to the side, much like a Myna bird, her dark eyes as cold as her tone.

Martha met and held the shopkeeper's gaze until finally the woman straightened both her head and her white cotton cap, atop an equally snowy mass of pinned curls. "It is a good morning, indeed, and I am grateful you are open."

The woman blinked. Normally, Martha kept her exchanges with the woman at a minimum, having become accustomed to the dour woman's habit of eyeing her as though she were a redcoat soldier from the Revolution invading and about to run off with her baked goods. This morning, however, during her devotions, Martha had been convicted to express appreciation where it was due. She should have thanked Hezekiah for his street sweeping. She would—next time she saw him.

Mrs. James pressed her hands on the counter. "Am I not open every day but the Lord's day?"

"Indeed." This was not going well, but God could do with it what He willed. Martha fished her folded bakery list from her bag. "Mrs. James, I have an order to place for Saturday next."

Myrtle shoved a broad hand toward Martha, and grabbed the paper. The woman raised it close to her face and scanned the images and numbers. The baker's wife couldn't read, so Martha had drawn pictures of what she wanted and the number next to it.

The plump elderly woman moved to her right, where the cases ended and there was an open bit of counter covered with spindles and completed orders. She laid the paper on the counter, picked up a short pencil, and bent over the list. "These are all the exact number, per usual, not dozens, is that right? I thought Dr. Osborne had taken over the dean's position while he's out with his wife's illness."

Martha puffed out a breath. "Yes, ma'am, just the usual. Father doesn't entertain as Dean Satterfield does." She really didn't appreciate the subtle reminder, in the woman's grating tone, that her father, although a university professor, didn't have a wide social circle. Even thirty years later, Americans were still stinging over the revolution and held little regard for a former Anglican priest.

What if, with the dean gone, more students and professors came, fearing to upset the man if he should return to find his event, in absentia, so poorly attended? How the currency within her purse could be stretched to cover father's latest attempt at attracting a suitor for her was beyond her understanding. But perhaps the dean hadn't expected Father to entertain. So was Father trying, for her stepmother's sake, to find Martha an intellectual man who didn't mind a wife who enjoyed reading, discussing philosophy, and periodically riding and jumping her horse over the magnificent hedges along the York River? She nibbled her lower lip. Of course, Father didn't know about the latter activity—unless her brother had told him.

"Chris came by and told me your mother was gone."

Chris? This woman referred to her brother Christopher as Chris? A muscle near her eye jumped. "Yes, my stepmother left with my younger sister to see her parents."

She simply could not refer to a woman only a decade older than herself as Mother, nor had Letitia requested that she or Christopher do so.

The door to the shop opened, the fresh air stirring the scents of flour, vanilla, and cinnamon and making Martha ravenous for one of the iced cinnamon buns displayed on the top counter.

Mrs. James eyed whoever walked in but then quickly returned her gaze to Martha. "And the boy? Johnny? What about him?"

Unbidden tears welled up in Martha's eyes and she blinked them back. Her youngest brother, her "pet", had been dispatched to boarding school in the farthest reaches of Yorktown. She couldn't make her mouth work to respond.

The baker slid the list back across the counter. "This is close to what Chris told me—and he's already paid, so don't you worry."

Martha sniffed. "My brother left a purchase list?" When she looked up, she could have sworn she saw genuine concern and compassion on the woman's face before Myrtle averted her gaze.

"Can I help you, sir?" Mrs. James called to the newcomer.

Slipping the paper back into her bag, Martha swiveled, keeping her eyes downcast. She mustn't think about Johnny being gone. She'd find a way to bring her little brother back home if it meant riding Galileo all the way to Yorktown and back by herself. Or convincing someone to take her by sloop, or schooner, down the river – but such a trip required money she didn't possess.

Martha glanced at the newcomer's cuffed and tailored steel-gray pants, ironed into a knife pleat that met expensive buffed, black leather boots similar to those her brother received from their grandfather the previous year. Curiosity overcame her desire to shield her face, which likely now sported a reddened nose and eyes from her tears. She looked up, catching the man's tailored vest and frock coat, a gleaming white shirt swathed with a navy and gold silk cravat tied loosely at his neck. His broad shoulders seemed peculiarly out of place with his face. For a moment she openly gaped at the man whose sculpted features, gleaming light green eyes, and golden hair had her questioning her sanity—was this the angel she'd prayed God would send her? The stranger was far too beautiful to be a real man. And with his immaculate appearance, how could he be real? Behind him, sunlight suddenly shone through the mullioned windows.

No, this being couldn't be mortal. Not with such a stunning appearance. She'd prayed for an angel to help her and she'd believed, but she hadn't expected to see a physical representation. What an encouragement from God that maybe one day she'd meet someone who didn't see her as an outcast. She beamed up at the heaven-sent visitor and then, laughing, she averted her gaze and went on her way, giddy with the joy of God's blessing her with an actual, tangible, manifestation of His holiness via an angelic being.

Her satin pumps barely touched the ground as Martha hurried home to thank God.

Phillip ran his hand along his smooth jawline as the bakery door closed behind the intriguing young woman. Intelligent pale eyes, the color of celadon, mesmerized him and belied her erratic, but almost winsome behavior. Her tinkling laugh didn't mock—it was strangely exhilarating, as though she'd issued some challenge to him. When she'd stared up at him so expectantly, his heart gave a tug, as though he was to do something for her—some assignment so important that all else must be tossed aside immediately. Then she'd fled.

The shopkeeper tapped the side of her silvery head with one pudgy finger. "Don't you worry any, she'd not escaped from our asylum."

"Ah." The thought hadn't crossed his mind, but now that she mentioned it... "Rather unusual behavior for a young lady."

The woman waved her hands dismissively. "The whole lot of them Osbornes are odd except her eldest brother. A secretive lot, they are."

Osborne. That was Johnny's surname. Was the flighty woman his mother? No, she was gone to England. This young woman was old enough to be Johnny's mother, though. Perhaps she was an aunt or an older cousin.

"I feel sorry for Miss Osborne, I do, but I never let it show. Doesn't bode well to have folks believin' you're soft hearted."

Phillip laughed. "Not in this business, madam, certainly!" He scanned the rows of muffins, biscuits, cookies, and breads and rolls. "A business can't run successfully if one was perpetually set upon by those wishing favors."

"Exactly." A tight smile unfurled as she looked up at him. This was a look he often received from older women. Mother claimed it was because they all wished they had a son as handsome as he was—to which he always scoffed. His elder brother was the handsome fellow, with dark hair that curled around his collar and flashing dark eyes and a charm that was as effortless as breathing. Little Johnny Osborne possessed similar coloring and had no doubt wrapped his older, book-reader sister around his little finger as George had done with all their nurses and nannies.

"I apologize for not introducing myself directly but I rather raced to get here…" He drew in a slow breath, thinking of how to explain who he was.

The proprietress's eyes widened and she glanced about the shop, as though someone might pop up from thin air. "Chris has told me all about it. Wait here." She turned, then parted blue and white checked curtains hanging from the door separating the front of the shop from the back.

He'd not even been able to finish his sentence to explain what he was there for. He didn't exactly represent Yorkview Academy, although he was there on business pertaining to the school.

In a moment, the homespun fabric panels separated again and she returned with a simple map, which she thrust at him. "There it is."

He glanced down. Williamsburg, Yorktown, and Gloucester were marked on the map, with the York River paralleling a squiggling line that terminated at the Episcopal church not far from the Yorktown docks. *How very odd.*

White head bobbing, the woman grinned. "I've wagered one week's worth of rolls for the school if Christopher wins. Which he will, of course."

"Rolls for the school?" he repeated.

"Yorkview School, where his brother attends."

Why would the young man, Christopher, want bread for the academy? "I am here to purchase some ginger cookies for that same school."

"Very good. I can see this race is already bringing me new business." She smiled, revealing small, uneven teeth.

"Well, how fortuitous for you. I've a need for ten dozen." His newest riding student, Johnny, craved the cookies, and cited Mrs. James' baked goods as the "very best in all of Virginia." And judging from the appearance of the beautiful young lady he'd met earlier, Williamsburg, and Mrs. James' shop, also held some of the loveliest creatures in Virginia.

Twin white eyebrows peaked. "Very good."

"I've some other business to conduct in Williamsburg while I'm here."

"Where do you live, sir?"

"I am Phillip Paulson, and…"

The woman gaped. "Of Paulson Farms?"

He ducked his chin.

Eyes wide, the woman scanned him from head to foot. "You're to race, sir?"

"Yes." How had that slipped from his mouth? Horrified, he tried to retract the word. *Lord, why do you allow my mouth to utter such deception?*

"Wish I could say I was happy for you, but I can't." She pursed her lips. "Don't see how those lads will have any chance against the likes of you— the best horseman in the Commonwealth, perhaps the entire seaboard. La!"

Drawing in a deep breath, he pulled to his full height, ready to disavow his word. "If Christopher fails, I promise you, madam, I shall set things to right. Your shop shan't suffer loss on my part. My participation is merely a lark." A lark? Since when did Phillip Lucien Paulson race his premier horses as a lark? Sweat broke out on his brow. He prided himself on his honesty and fairness and now here he was misleading this woman. A man's honor wasn't to be trifled with.

Was that a blush flowering beneath her powdered cheeks? It was. "You are a gentleman, sir."

"Please keep this our little secret, madam."

She shrugged. "What harm can come of those boys not knowing your intent, Mr. Paulson?"

"None." He smiled broadly. He had no intention of racing in whatever Christopher and his friends were doing, which was no doubt all in good sport. And apparently for a good cause. Father and his cronies had been encouraging him to set up an equestrian academy, of sorts, for nearly two years and now that he had done so, at his brother's school, they acted as though Phillip was a complete imbecile. The older men's veiled comments and secretive meetings had increased and the time had come for him to invite himself to attend. But with esteemed men, some of whom had served in both the French-Indian wars as mere youths as well as the Revolution, one did not invite oneself in among their august company even if one was the son of a member.

"I can bag those cookies up for you now or you can return later to collect them."

"Thank you, madam." He scanned the shelves laden with sweet buns, Sarah Lund bread, and scones. If he'd tried to bring any of these home to Paulson Estates, Cook would have his hide. But a few more for his students couldn't hurt, and the school cook was already overburdened and wouldn't protest. "Please add as many sweet rolls as you have available to the order. I'll return for them after my visit with Professor Osborne, if you could direct me to his home." The headmaster kept his address list to himself, and since Johnny didn't reside at one of the many plantations the other boys occupied, it had proved a large task to locate the man's residence. The child didn't know what street he lived on.

"Why, you just met the professor's daughter." She pointed to the door. "That was Johnny and Chris's sister."

Chapter 2

At the rear of the Osborne property, in their minuscule Anglican chapel, a place forbidden by the Commonwealth for worship, Martha knelt on red velvet cushions. Had the strikingly handsome blond man been the answer to her previous prayer? If so, what was to come of their encounter? Had God allowed her a glimpse to her guardian angel to encourage her? If so, God had a perverse sense of humor, for now Martha berated herself for being attracted to the celestial being. It wasn't right to have such reactions toward an angel! Instead of being intent on praying about her brother she had come home, prostrated herself, and thought only of the impressive figure her angel had made and not of what had inspired her fervent prayer for help from on high.

Ever since Martha's last conversation with her stepmother—an argument over Johnny—she'd been troubled in her spirit. Letitia had proclaimed before her departure to England, "*If* Emily and I return," then had hastily amended her statement to, "*When* we return, there shall be changes in this household."

At the time, Martha had interpreted Letitia's words as a veiled threat—as though saying she'd stay in England if Martha continued to voice her opinion about Johnny. Now, though, with many weeks gone by, Martha couldn't help but wonder if Stepmother meant something else, instead. *God, if so, please show me what to do.*

Was Martha's plan to leave her home and establish herself in a small business so far-fetched? Although society might frown upon such a decision, she and her family were already outcasts.

If Martha moved out, then Father and Letitia would have their privacy. There would still be visits with Johnny, Christopher, and Emily. There would be only one adult woman in the household, which would hopefully tamp down some of Letitia's ongoing temper tantrums whenever Martha had done anything in the house not meeting her standards. Poor father. And what must the boys think? Emily merely smirked and kept quiet. Would she become Stepmother's new target? Martha drew in a long slow breath of the dusty incense scent that cloaked the sanctuary. Dear Lord, how would her father and stepmother manage? Neither directed the household but left those tasks to Martha. She slowly stood, stretched, and pressed a hand to her lower back. She still had no peace about her plan. Martha recollected the concern and patient interest reflected in the angel's eyes. God did know her needs. He would surely provide.

At the sound of the door creaking open, she whirled around. Her brother's former friend, Graham Tarleton, stood in the doorway, his legs braced in a wide stance. A cocky child, he'd grown even more irksome in adulthood. Fawned over by his parents and the young ladies of Williamsburg, the handsome young buck thought far more of himself than a gentleman ought.

"What are you doing here, Graham?" The sunlight from the stained glass windows dimmed as he took two strides forward. Martha shivered and rubbed her elbows. "Christopher isn't here."

"Not looking for Chris." Graham and Christopher had a tentative truce in their argument over a girl. During Emily's departure dinner, Graham Tarleton's mooning eyes had been fixed upon her sister.

Where were their servants? How had Graham passed into their backyard without notice? "Emily has left with Mother." But Graham already knew this. She cringed. And instead of taking Johnny to see his maternal grandparents in England, he'd been left at a boarding school across the river.

Graham scowled. "Should I care?"

But the slight slump in his shoulders and the twitch of a muscle in his jaw belied his words. So Graham indeed had become interested by her fourteen-year-old sister's flirtatious manner. No wonder Letitia had changed her mind and transported Emily with her. "Of course not—Emily is still very young."

A wicked grin spread across his face. How had her brother's friend hardened into such a troubled young man? And why had Christopher forgiven him so readily when Miranda Lightfoot had been the light in his own eyes for over a year before Graham had stolen her away?

"You're not." His eyelids lowered to half-mast and remained there, causing her to shiver.

"In any event, I've already said my prayers. You're welcome to the use of the chapel." Martha took two steps toward him with the intention of getting around and out.

"Our families have been friends for a very long time." A salacious look altered his fine features.

"Until you and Christopher argued."

He shrugged. "All is forgiven now."

"Is it?" Christopher had been less and less talkative since he'd taken ill the previous month.

"Indeed, and our families will resume an even closer friendship."

She sighed and gave him an arched look. "How so?" The Tarletons had taken up intimately with the Osbornes before Letitia and Father had courted. Although the British-born Tarletons had been friends of the family when mother was yet alive, that relationship primarily consisted of the two matrons enjoying fox hunts with a group of ladies in Charles City.

"Didn't your stepmother speak with you?" He moved closer. "Before she left?"

Needles of fear prickled her neckline. "About?"

"Us." He grasped her arm tightly and jerked Martha toward him.

"Let go!" She averted her head and tried to twist away but his fingers bit into her shoulders.

"Or what?" He hissed. "Didn't Letitia tell you things would be changing around here? A great deal?"

The crack of wood on stone caused them both to jump. Graham released her as her angel from the bakery strode forward into the light. His eyes locked with hers, sending a frisson of electricity through her as he tossed half of a broken wooden staff aside. Her rescuer barreled toward Graham, arm uplifted. "Touch the lady again and I shall be forced to lay the remainder of this cane across your back."

"You wouldn't dare…"

Fire seemed to flare from the golden-haired stranger's eyes, leaving no doubt that he would keep his word. "Don't try my patience!"

A muscle in Graham's jaw twitched and his eyelids lowered, giving him a sinister appearance. She shivered.

Her avenger gestured toward the back door. "Into your home, Miss Osborne, and away from the likes of this devil."

Martha hesitated.

Graham took one half step toward her protector.

But when arm muscles bulged beneath the man's overcoat, and knuckles whitened around the staff, a gape-mouthed Graham fled the sanctuary.

She didn't even know this man, yet he defended her. Maybe that was because the stranger truly was an angel. Her avenging angel.

"Go inside, Miss, and keep the doors barred." He brushed particles of dust from his vest as he slowly surveyed the small chapel.

Martha grabbed a fistful of her skirt and hurried into the house as fast as her satin slippers allowed, her heart still hammering from Graham's insolence and the attack that had almost occurred.

"Missy, stop!" Dicey, her arms full of bedclothes, stopped Martha before she collided with her.

After she turned from the laundress, Martha pulled the wooden slat into place on the back door. "Keep the doors barred for now, please."

"Missy?"

"Just do as I say! Do the wash later." Martha hated the pique in her voice and worse yet the tears that suddenly streamed down her face as she fled up to her bedroom, grasping the bannister as she went. She couldn't have Dicey going in and out of the laundry building if Graham lurked nearby.

Throwing herself down on her counterpane coverlet, Martha took quick breaths. What was Graham Tarleton speaking about? She had her own plans for a life, which didn't include him. When father spoke about things changing, as he rarely did, it was always in hushed tones with other professors in the Philosophy Department, and in reference to concerns about the British navy. How many times had they railed against the kidnapping of their young men from American shores and forcing them to fight against Napoleon? And why did such an unrelated thought suddenly occur when thinking of Graham and Letitia? *Am I losing my mind?*

No. Just listen. And obey.

That still, small voice had gotten harder to hear until recently, when it seemed all manner of irrational thoughts were coming to her.

Still. He was Lord.

Yes, Lord, Thy will be done.

In his effort to restrain himself from pummeling young Tarleton, sweat soaked through Phillip's linen shirt, vest, and jacket. He couldn't very well knock on the professor's door and explain to him that he'd booted a friend of the family from their property, if, as the insouciant man claimed and as the baker had asserted, the lout was indeed Christopher Osborne's college friend. Once again, Phillip had been foiled by Tarleton. It stirred a burning in his gut over what had happened with his cousin Miranda, now removed to the far reaches of Norfolk on the other side of the peninsula. Because of schedule at the academy, Phillip couldn't get back to Williamsburg for at least another week. Blasted Tarleton. Not only had that, but Phillip's favorite walking cane now lain atop the Osborne's refuse pile.

Heaving a sigh, he loosened his cravat and made his way up the side street away from the Osborne's home and toward the market. Brick buildings alternated with some of the newer wooden structures going up along the main venue. With America building up a new nation, he could almost smell the scent of progress in the sawdust and whitewash-scented air.

Phillip turned from the Osborne's quiet lane and onto the hard-packed crushed tabby walkway. At least the weather hadn't been wet and he didn't have to dodge any puddles while wearing his best dress shoes. He'd wanted to look the part of a town gentleman and not a country horse breeder who was

31

at the mercy of his father and brother for his livelihood. What would Phillip do if Father died and George evicted him and his horses from the Paulson Farm's stables?

In a short while he'd reached the edge of the market street.

"Fresh crabs! Best in Virginia!" The scent of seafood emanated from a nearby fishmonger's stall.

Several slave women stopped at the cart. Their bright head coverings shone a bit of brightness in the sea of dark clothing worn by the businessmen who strode by.

Walkers moved aside as a carriage, drawn by a pair of perfectly matched bays, drove by. From within, Graham Tarleton's father sat erect, his demeanor suggestive of a man who would be king if such was possible in a free land. How Phillip would relish beating the man's son when he raced against him.

He strode on toward the bakery, where the scent of sugar and vanilla bean overpowered the fishy odors he left behind.

Inside, several young bucks clustered near the counter, elbow to suited elbow.

"We raced through the crowd to get here, Mrs. James," a redheaded youth proclaimed.

The other gents laughed, but Phillip frowned, failing to understand their humor. The pack of them huddled together, reminding him of pups about to be tossed a few cornbread scraps from the kitchen.

The woman nodded, turned on her heel, and went to the rear of the store. Soon the baker handed each what appeared to be the same map he'd received earlier. So that was why she'd retrieved the diagram for him earlier—Phillip had accidentally spoken their coded phrase of racing to the bakery.

Mrs. James opened her now-empty palm to them. "There's a sugar cookie to be paid for, young fellows, for each of you."

After each young man placed a coin into her calloused hands, the elderly baker removed cookies from her case and gave each one.

As they departed, they returned their hats to their heads and tipped their brims at Phillip. He recognized all as being elder brothers to his academy students, all sons of large plantation owners and close to a decade younger than himself. He dipped his chin as they passed and then moved to join the proprietress.

"Good day, madam. I've returned."

She arched a white eyebrow. "My eyes are just fine, Mr. Paulson. I can see you've come back. And I might say, you waited quite patiently for a man of your station."

"Thank you. I think." He chuckled. "Mrs. James, do you know if Tarleton has retrieved his map?"

"Ah, yes, he and Christopher are thick as thieves again – now that a girl isn't coming between them." She nodded for emphasis, set a loaf of Sally Lunn inside the case, and then wiped her hands on her apron. "Never knew who the girl was, only that they both wanted her for themself but she preferred young Master Tarleton. Then she left them both."

They referred to Miranda as a girl? True, his cousin wasn't quite a woman, but she was, or had been, a sweet, innocent young lady and not someone to be referred to so flippantly. And how had she kept the courtship with Osborne secret? From what it appeared today, Tarleton was now chasing after Miss Osborne. Now not only would Phillip endeavor to have Johnny returned to his family home but to somehow keep Miss Osborne safe from the likes of Tarleton. He knew only too well what the young rake was capable of where young women were involved.

"I see. And where is this doubly-pursued young lady now?" Thank God Mrs. James didn't realize the "girl" was the daughter of his Uncle Lightfoot. Wouldn't her tongue wag over that?

"Heard she left for Norfolk—probably chasing after a sea captain now. Graham says a college boy wasn't good enough for her."

So the two young men had quarreled over his cousin. And now Tarleton was spreading rumors that she was chasing a bigger catch. Phillip knew without a doubt that Christopher Osborne wasn't responsible for Miranda's condition, for his terrified cousin had revealed her situation to him alone. Phillip hadn't known that his cousin and Osborne had ever officially courted, which only meant their liaisons must have been clandestine as had been the contact with Tarleton. That the cad had the audacity to abandon Uncle Lightfoot's youngest daughter in her time of need and now chase after his friend's sister. Surely if young

Osborne was the culprit his sweet cousin would have told him. He trusted her utterly.

Phillip rubbed his chin. "I'm no sea captain, nor a college boy, and well past such tittle tattle, but I'd best catch my packet home." Before this budding headache blossomed into full bloom.

"A brisk breeze today, you should make good progress."

"If you hear of anything that concerns you about Miss Osborne, would you send word to me at my home?" He slid money across the counter, enough to ensure her interest and keep her silent.

Although she attempted to be surreptitious in counting the money, the woman's eyes widened. She began to cough and patted her ample bosom, presumably because of the amount he'd set down. Although he wasn't always so generous, Phillip had set out a goodly sum to procure the baker's powers of observation. No other young woman should suffer as Miranda had.

"Are you all right?" He pulled out his handkerchief and handed it to the shopkeeper.

Mrs. James covered her mouth and nodded. When she ceased her episode, she slid the cash into a drawer. "You can be sure I'll keep close watch over Martha, and I'll get word to you."

"Thank you." He turned to go.

"Mr. Paulson?"

"Yes?"

"You'll be back for the Osborne's party Saturday eve next, won't you?" The singsong quality of her voice left no doubt that she suspected he knew nothing of it, which he didn't.

He hesitated only a moment. And before he could deny it, he said, "Yes, I shall."

What on earth was coming over him? Twice in one day he'd uttered falsehoods. *Lord forgive me, again. I shan't be racing in those young men's race nor shall I be attending a party to which I am not invited.*

Several hours later, after disembarking from the Paulson schooner and retrieving his mount from the stable, Phillip tried to shake off the image of Tarleton setting upon Miss Osborne. Now, not only did he have concerns about Johnny, but distress over the notion of that fiend preying upon a single woman who defied society's conventions by wandering around town unescorted. His head began to pound as he mounted Othello and patted the gelding's glossy black head.

"Good boy. Take me home, old fellow." Would he ever have a place that was his very own home? While it was clear that Paulson Farms would always be his residence while his father was alive, could the same be said when George became master of the property? And would he keep the farm operational without resorting to slaves as their uncle Dodd, on his huge estate, continued to do? Andrée's family still expressed outrage that their family initially refused the gift of "property" they'd sent with their daughter—a maid, an additional footman and a valet for George, an additional kitchen servant, and a stable lad no older than Johnny Osborne. Mother had finally relented when the slave child's mother was also allowed to come. And Father consulted an attorney as to how to set the slaves free within the Commonwealth, so they may have their freedmen papers.

Instead of riding toward the farm, Phillip directed Othello toward the school. Reading stories to the lads each night had begun to establish a routine he could not ignore. Phillip had always been a creature of habit, but this new regimen had taken root so fast, it astonished him. He could not envision himself sleeping soundly until he'd ensured Johnny had been read to properly.

Othello nickered to the other horses as they arrived at the stable. Phillip dismounted and passed his reins to a stablehand.

"Mr. Phillip!" Johnny ran across the lawn, away from a small group of boys tossing rings.

Home. How could a parent leave such a child behind? A boy who inspired such a ready attachment? Who brought up emotions only connected to permanence? And to a home.

Why, when he considered that notion, did Martha Osborne's pretty face come to mind?

Chapter 3

After awaking from a night filled with dreams of the angel Gabriel doing battle with a host of red-eyed monstrous black stallions, Martha awoke expecting to find the stranger standing over her bed. When she didn't, she went about her morning ablutions. Pulling her robe tightly around her, she'd snuck into Christopher's room and found him yet soundly asleep. At least he wasn't coughing. But his room reeked of brandy. Was his "illness" a ploy to get himself into his cups without Father objecting to his frequent tavern visits? She stifled a groan of disgust and returned to her room.

Martha donned her riding attire and soon scrambled down to the stables, ready for a taste of freedom. Christopher, in the state she found him, would likely sleep until noon, giving her plenty of time for riding. She went straight to the stall as the steed nickered to her in greeting.

"Galileo, how could anyone neglect so beautiful a beast as you?" Martha rubbed the gelding's back. "Christopher is sleeping in, yet again, and here you need a splendid run, don't you?"

"Miss Martha, you gonna get in some big trouble one of these days if your father finds out." The tall, lanky freedman, Asa, shook his head as he helped her lead the gelding out.

"Make sure Father doesn't know, then." She grinned at their stablehand. "Now give me a lift."

In short order, she directed Galileo out behind the chapel and through their neighbor's grove at the edge of Williamsburg proper. Keeping to the paths, she could avoid detection as she headed south. Before long she was on the horse path to Yorktown. Ten miles was a long jaunt, especially over the terrain she had to cover, but the weather looked promising, with robin's egg blue skies and clouds like puffs of drifting cotton bolls.

How she wished the angelic stranger rode beside her. She took comfort knowing God was always with her. But wouldn't it be lovely to draw strength from the physical presence of a protecting man? A man who accepted her as she was and didn't try to mold her into someone else, like Letitia had tried, and failed to do.

She exhaled a long sigh, bent low over Galileo, and pushed him to a canter as they entered open fields. A network of her friend's plantations allowed her to travel unimpeded, save for several short jaunts.

Just as Martha gave Galileo his head, someone or something crashed through the thicket beside her.

"Marty!" A youthful voice called out.

Martha's heart hammered as she slowed Galileo to a halt. He neighed in protest.

Sally King's younger tow-headed brother urged his mare toward her. "Marty! I need a favor!"

He drew alongside her with a lopsided grin. At fourteen, he already sported the beginning of a moustache.

"What is it, Nathan?"

"Please convince Christopher that I can race." He puffed out his narrow chest as though to prove his point, but failed. "I'm old enough."

"Shouldn't you be at the college?"

"I'm sick." He faked a cough and pounded a fist against his chest.

Had Nathan, as well as her brother, concocted a scheme to convince their families they were ill, yet they were, in fact, well but carrying out their own plans? "What are you up to?"

"I'm practicing. I want to do the race with them."

"What race?"

"The one to the steeple of Grace Episcopal!"

"Tell me all about it and I'll see what I can do. But no promises!"

Nathan prattled on until Martha's ears were ringing and her head swimming. "Whoever wins gets a large cash prize."

"How much?"

When Nathan named the amount, Martha gasped. Such a sum would surely cover a goodly deposit on the livery she hoped to run and rent for the cottage adjacent to the stables.

Galileo munched on grass while the youth explained Christopher's race. "We're supposed to get from Bruton Parish to Grace Episcopal as quickly as we can. No rules about the route we take, but I suppose with all those maps Chris has made for the college, he has an advantage."

"So the rules are limited?"

"Right." Again he straightened, led his horse in a tight circle, and announced, "I believe we're all young gents and shan't cheat and what not."

"Are there any rules against ladies competing?" She arched an eyebrow at him.

With Christopher so ill recently might he even be able to ride?

"Dunno." He scrunched his small features together, reminding her of a dried apple's head doll's face. "But I doubt it."

If she won, and began a new life, surely then she could bring Johnny home. "Thank you, Nathan. I shall put in a good word for you."

Phillip's manservant, Mingo, eyed him quizzically. "Ya sure ya don' want me to come with ya, sir?"

"Uncle's footman, Benjamin, can square me away once I arrive."

The tall man shook his head and mumbled something as he finished buffing Phillip's shoes to a high glossy shine.

A rap on the door was followed by Father's bushy mane and a servant standing behind him. "Solomon told me you were dressing for courting, but I wouldn't have believed it had I not witnessed this with my own eyes."

"Solomon should be looking for a new job." Phillip narrowed his eyes, catching the thin, grizzled-haired servant's wide, dark eyes before he disappeared down the hall.

Father chuckled. He turned his head and called out, "No need to hurry off, Solomon, my son isn't paying the bills around here. Not yet." His voice dropped off to deadly quiet on the last two words and Phillip locked gazes with him.

He frowned. When, if ever, would he be issuing orders or paying bills at the estate? George would have that task. Phillip looked away, taking in the finely appointed room he'd called his own ever since he'd left the nursery. Checkered homespun curtains and American-made furnishings clashed with *Maman*'s massive French armoire from Paris that hunkered in one corner of the room.

Father closed the door behind himself as he left. At least he knew when to quit agitating. Mingo, however, took up tssking.

"If'n ya had give this vest to me earlier I'd have brushed it out right good. But now…"

"It's all right, Mingo. I'll have Benjamin give it a good airing and brush it out before I…" What should Phillip call what he was about to do? He wasn't an invited guest. On rare occasions, some of the local gentry showed up at any social gathering without an invitation and the hosts chose to overlook their social gaffe. Would the Osbornes do the same?

"Leastwise ya sit down heah and let me fix your hair for ya." The servant waved toward a Louis XIV chair near the window and Phillip grunted as he lowered himself into it.

"I need my hair tied back in a queue for riding." Although the strip of old leather that secured it could do with replacing.

"Yahsir, I know you think so."

But with a jerk and a few snips, Phillip's long shank of hair fell to the floor. He rose to his feet, his hands involuntarily balling into fists. When Mingo shrank back, Phillip flexed his fingers, as air stabbed around his naked neck. "What have you done?"

The man's lips trembled as he slowly lowered his hands, which had flown up in a defensive posture. "Bringing ya into the nineteenth century, Mr. Phillip."

Pressing his eyes closed, Phillip prayed for patience. When he opened them, Mingo held a mirror out and Phillip took it, examining the damage. "My hair was perfectly fine."

"Yahsir, it was…" Mingo's lips pulled into an amused pucker. "For old folk, mebbe."

"I say!" True, Phillip was set in his own ways. "Mayhaps more backcountry gentleman than city, but I've no desire to look like old Boney." His mother might be French but there was little love for Napoleon Bonaparte, nor his hairstyles in this household.

"No, sir. But we could fix you up here, a little." He pointed around Phillip's hairline.

Phillip slumped back into the chair. Might Miss Osborne find a more current style appealing? Would she cease staring at him as though he was some strange creature? Perhaps if he no longer had his hair so severely tied back with a leather strip

43

then she may consider him more of a gentleman—instead of a stranger who'd so heavy-handedly tried to evict a family friend from her property.

"Keep going, Mingo. Make me pretty." He laughed. This young woman didn't seem to know who he was. Perhaps he'd keep it that way. After he spoke to her father, he'd chat with her alone about Johnny. And about his position at the academy. There was no need to share anything else unless someone there recognized him and tried to make conversation. He'd ensure such an event didn't happen.

All Martha could think about, as she prepared for the party, was the race. One with a large sum of money for a winner. And if she won, she could purchase a small stable at the edge of town and rent a cottage where perhaps she and Johnny could wait out Letitia's return. *Would she return?* Martha nibbled her lower lip as she sliced carrots on a wide chopping block, brushing the ends off and into a tall crock destined for the neighbor's pigs, once it was filled.

Jessamine, a pretty servant with a café au lait complexion, slanted one eyebrow at Martha. "You choppin' with a little too much gusto, there, Missy Martha. Mebbe you should slow down afore you chop off one of those pritty little fingahs of your'n."

"I'm fine." She set her knife down and wiped her hands on her apron.

"Don' you need to get ready for the party, Missy?"

She'd not really considered all the physical preparations she needed to make, but she should have. All Martha had to do tonight, she'd convinced herself, was to begin her ruse for the race. And that meant she needed to convince Christopher's friends that she was one of the most feminine and scatter-brained females in all of the Tidewater area. For if she was to take his place in the race, she couldn't have them contemplating that she'd consider such a proposition. At least half of his friends already judged her of dull wits. Convincing those young bucks that she was also decidedly female shouldn't be so hard. After all, hadn't Father and Christopher both professed that men thought with their eyes and wanted to believe what they saw, particularly when it came to pretty women? At this point, dressed in her work clothes, Martha certainly wasn't feeling very attractive. But that would be remedied.

Martha surveyed the kitchen house where the flurry of activity preceded their party. The number of attendees had swelled from only a dozen invited to nearly forty, when somehow the young men began asking others to attend Father's first party in the dean's absence. Her pile of carrots now filled an entire gallon bowl for Cook to prepare.

"I found more preserves and fruit in the cellar, Miss." Hannah, their senior-most kitchen servant, displayed a crock of strawberry jam and dried apples.

"Wonderful." Her stepmother had deferred to Martha in matters of the kitchen and she'd requested extra fruit set up that year for just such a possible event. Father never bothered with household expenses other than asking that she make sure all the bills were kept up to date, which they were.

Someone rapped on the doorframe to the white-washed building behind the house and Martha slowly turned, afraid she'd see Graham sullenly standing there. Instead, a swarthy man of middling years clutched a crate of what appeared to be cider to his homespun vest.

"Hard cider and light cider from Shirley Plantation, miss. Shall I lay it here?"

Hannah waved her hand toward the bricked floor beneath the open shelving on the back wall. "Over there, please."

After finishing his task the man handed her a note. "You can read, miss?"

Both her father and mother had tutored her at home. "Oh, yes, please tell Mr. and Mrs. Carter a sincere thank you." How long had it been since she'd participated in foxhunts at their estate? Since before Mother died. She'd received notes periodically from the family, a few from William, who must now be a young man and not the child whose antics she once enjoyed.

She scanned the note's contents, and it was signed in Mrs. Carter's fine penmanship with an invitation for her to come visit sometime. She smiled to herself, her heart warming. "This is the fifth plantation to send us felicitations and spirits or the contents for fruit punch."

"Them young men gonna cause a commotion if you give 'em too much of that hard cider, Miss

Martha." Hannah's features tightened in disapproval.

The porter laughed as he tipped his hat and departed.

One long rectangular table was covered with sausages, tarts, fruit to be cut for trays, and cheese.

Jessamine caught Martha's eye. "You best get dressed, Miss Martha, if you gonna be ready for tonight. You leave this all to us now, ya hear?"

Despite her nerves being wound so tight they might snap like frayed cording, Martha repeated The Lord's Prayer, hoping for some of God's peace to come over her. For naught. Surely He approved her plan to enter the race and win the prize. For if she did so, Martha would have a way to retrieve her brother from school as well as have funds to purchase a small stall for livery or stables at the edge of Duke of Gloucester Street.

Martha paced the floor of her room, the sounds of men's laughter carrying up from downstairs. The hurriedly hired musicians tuned their stringed instruments, the long plaintive note of the violin catching her strained emotions and carrying them out her open window. She moved to the creamy muslin-curtained lead-paned aperture and surveyed the back courtyard. Movement near the stables caught her eye. Had she glimpsed a tawny headed man astride a chestnut horse?

"Pooh." She tapped her fan against her cheek. Everywhere she'd been the previous week, she'd been sure she'd caught sight of the handsome man from the bakery. He was of an age beyond university studies and wasn't a professor, for she'd met them all. And not a friend of her brother's, either.

And what did it matter, anyway, because all the young men who'd called on her were disinclined to court a young woman who possessed her own opinion, particularly on the matters of education and law. She huffed out a sigh. At least she had the use of Galileo—for now.

Dicey helped Martha into her fancy undergarments and secured her corset. "Not too tight, Missy?"

"It's fine." She lifted her arms as the servant lowered her peach silk dress around her, its top layer fluttering around her.

After adjusting the cap sleeves, and tying them off, Dicey tied the long taupe satin ribbon beneath Martha's empire-waisted gown. "You look deep in thought, Miss Martha."

"Do you think I look...womanly?" She tapped one long finger on her leg as she reviewed her plan. *If I am going to throw those young men off my scent, I must be the most feminine of young ladies tonight. I can and I shall.*

"You be the prettiest lady heah, that's for sure." Dicey motioned for Martha to sit on her velvet upholstered boudoir chair.

The servant arranged Martha's tresses into coils and secured them with glittering paste clips. When completed, Dicey nestled a small tiara of Mother's into Martha's curls. Long strands trailed down the low cut of her gown. "Do you think this bodice is modest enough?"

Dicey snorted softly. "Compared to what them French ladies now wearin' when they be in Washington City—I sure think so."

All of the newspapers, even the Williamsburg Gazette, had reported the French vistors' scandalous attire.

"I can't imagine any of our Williamsburg ladies imitating the Frenchwomen's provocative, sheer gowns."

The pretty young woman laughed. "And if they did, my oh my—how would those stories carry!"

"Very true." Although no longer the capital of Virginia, Williamsburg was no small backwater town and the Tidewater area carried a brisk commerce on the seaboard. "Not that I'd ever consider such a thing myself." Not even if it meant that she blinded the young men present with her attributes to the extent that when she took her brother's place for the race, they'd never notice it wasn't he.

Why, why, why did it have to be this way? Why should I have to treat Christopher's tiresome young friends and father's university cronies as though I am enchanted by them?

"Mmmm, mmmm, mmmm, you sure lookin' as pretty as the Missus tonight." The servant cocked her head to the side and rearranged several curls.

How did her stepmother manage flirting so easily? "I wish flattery and small talk came to me as naturally as they do to Letitia."

"Makin' big eyes, leanin' in close, and actin' like every man is the finest in Virginia—why that comes as easy to the Missus as breathin'!"

That was it! Martha would imitate Letitia's mannerisms and ways, but not overly so—she didn't need to be construed as mocking her stepmother nor trying to solicit too much male attention of the unwanted kind. Such as Graham's. A quick image of her stepmother's face scrunched in concentration passed through Martha's mind. Letitia had the habit of immediately burning any missives she received. And unlike when she was in a man's company, if Martha came upon her whilst she was reading her letters, she was quickly and rudely sent on her way with a reprimand. But Martha had held her tongue and not returned the woman's vitriolic words to her.

I shall hold my tongue. I have much practice. I shall smile all night and laugh at Christopher's friends' inane comments. I shall bat my eyelashes and fan myself as I look up at each young buck as if he alone is the handsomest man at the party.

If Christopher's chums considered Martha to be a flower of utmost femininity, then when she arrived at their race, they'd *never* suspect it was Martha, not Christopher, on Galileo.

Her hands trembled as Dicey assisted her with her gloves. For the first time in her life, she was tempted to sneak to her father's office and partake of a goblet of port before facing the crowd downstairs. She pressed her eyes shut. *Dear God, you know I am opinionated, too educated for a woman's own good, and my temper isn't quite as tame as it should be, but if you see fit to change me, do so now—but not enough that I should put aside my desire to win the race, in Jesus's name, Amen.*

A rap on the door preceded Jessamine's entrance. "Miss Martha, they're expectin' ya downstairs. Are ya ready?"

Jessamine sucked in a breath. "Oh my. Ain't ya the spittin' image of your mother when she was of yer age, miss."

Dicey stifled a giggle. "Wouldn't Lady Letitia spit nails if she could see who the loveliest Osborne lady was now?"

Martha cringed at Dicey's reference to her stepmother as Lady Letitia. In America, one did not use such titles. But she bit her lip. "Thank you. I'll be down in a minute."

Giving Martha a curtsy, Jessamine backed out of the room and Dicey affixed glittering earbobs to Martha's ear lobes and then wrapped one of her mother's jeweled necklaces around her neck.

"I think you ready now, Missy."

"Yes. Thank you."

Drawing in a sustaining breath, Martha pasted a smile on her face and exited her room. She descended the stairway, the satiny smooth curved walnut rail comforting beneath her fingertips. This was her home. But not for much longer. She and Johnny could make other plans. And the sad thing was—her stepmother and her father would only give weak protest over how "unseemly" it would be. That was, if Letitia did return. And that niggling recurring voice seemed more of the Holy Spirit than of Martha's own wishes. If she had her own desire,

Letitia and Father would love the boy much more than either of them had ever demonstrated.

Head high, shoulders back, stomach tucked in, Martha continued on into the main salon.

A half dozen of her brother's friends casually glanced up, but then their eyes widened and several of them momentarily gaped. She couldn't resist the tiny smirk that tugged at her lips, but quickly regained her composure. *I am the princess coming to court, and these are my suitors from the far off lands of the realm.* Not likely, since she'd known most of them since they were children attending day school with Christopher in Williamsburg.

That thought made her frown, because Johnny wouldn't be there. Instead, her younger brother had been shuffled off to a boarding school, away from family and friends. One of the young men, Bryce Evans, took several steps toward her and then hesitated, scanning her face. *No, no, I mustn't think any negative thoughts.* She quickly put a smile back on and held out her hand to the barrister's son.

"Why Miss Osborne, I've never seen you looking so beautiful."

She dipped her chin slightly, then looked up from beneath fluttering eyelashes. Goodness, this might make her dizzy. She wobbled slightly and Bryce took her elbow.

"Are you quite all right? Come, let's find you a seat."

"Oh, no, that's fine." She couldn't sit or she'd have trouble convincing each guest that he was the most superior male on the planet. "I'm afraid your rather grown-up handsome appearance has simply flustered me."

Was that a blush spreading across his high cheekbones? It was. *Victory.*

He laughed. "May I procure some punch for you?"

"Delightful." Because then she could move on to another target.

As soon as Bryce moved away, she opened her fan, trying to remember what all those silly fan gestures meant, but unable to come up with a single notion. As gracefully as she could, she meandered through the crush of gentlemen toward the savories table, the scent of ham biscuits and thyme wafting toward her. A dark-haired man, about forty, one of the new professors, stepped into her path. "Miss Osborne, so nice to see you again. I was hoping we could continue our conversation about Newton and his theories."

Throwing back her head, she laughed in what she hoped sounded bubbly and ebullient. "Why, Dr. Gredler, this is a party." Not that similar events kept her from discussing philosophy and the like. But for tonight...

She cast him a sidelong glance then moved off toward a cluster of three of Christopher's older university friends. "Gentlemen, welcome."

The trio swiveled toward her.

"This cannot be Martha Osborne." The tallest of the three, the favorite bachelor of Williamsburg, swooped in like an eagle to its nest.

Chapter 4

Blast. Phillip had no chance against the eldest Tyler heir, a handsome rake with dark hair that curled around his pristine white collar.

Phillip's own head felt naked with so much of his hair cut away and that curling around his face itched and irritated. Blasted Mingo. Why had he allowed him to chop off his hair? Because of Martha Osborne. That was why and the reason for him hiding here in the shadows gawking at the young lady. When had she transformed from the beautiful, albeit odd duck, he'd met at the bakery, into this full-on flirtatious belle? It made him almost dazed to consider what had brought on such an alteration. Was she in desperate straits to obtain a suitor? According to little Johnny, she "doesn't want to be someone's dull old wife shoved off in a corner, she wants to be free like boys are—like me." Poor little chap shed a few tears over his final words, as he was cordoned off from society more fully than even his sister.

Martha Osborne flitted from one young man to another, maneuvering her fan with skill he'd only witnessed in the grand halls of Europe. And what was the meaning of that tap against her chin? Was she encouraging the middle-aged man to call upon her privately? Would such a pedantic type even know what signal she was sending? What an idiot he'd been, thinking he'd speak with her alone when she'd just sent the message to at least three men that she was willing to entertain them absent of company.

He swiped at the irritating curls on his forehead. Surely it was his hair irritating him and not all the attention Martha received. He needed to stop obsessing over the lovely young woman. His intent had been to speak with the lady's father about his young son and to learn more about the upcoming secret race, wasn't it?

A servant carrying a tray of ham biscuits backed up into Phillip. "Sorry, sir."

"Not at all your fault. I'm looking for Professor Osborne."

"He's not here, sir."

"Is he not the host of this event?"

"Yes, sir, but he's in his office." The man's interaction with him was attracting attention.

"Thank you." Phillip edged away from the servant and along the perimeter of the rectangular room and then moved into the corridor, whose flocked wallpaper was one he'd seen in the palace when last his family had journeyed to London with Uncle Lightfoot on one of his purchasing trips. Spying lamplight from a cracked door that led to a room located near the front of the home, which was an ideal location for an office, Phillip hesitated; he listened for conversation to indicate the professor may be inside the room. A man was humming an Irish parlor tune; one George and his mother enjoyed playing on the piano at home. Phillip tapped on the paneled door.

"Enter!" A vigorous male voice called out.

Phillip opened the door and entered a square room cluttered with books, stacks of papers, and framed botanical prints. Centered on the far wall, suspended between two uncurtained mullioned windows, was a surprisingly large silver cross that would seem more fitting in a sanctuary. But hadn't young Johnny maintained that his father had been an Anglican priest? Not that there was employment for such in America. The faint scent of sandalwood and coffee comingled with the remnants of ever-present woodsmoke.

"Good day, sir, or rather good eve to you."

The man within remained seated at his desk, but angled his head. "I'm sorry, but while you look familiar, I'm afraid I don't recognize you, young man."

"Forgive me. I am Phillip Paulson of Paulson Farms, and we met briefly when you brought your son to my brother's academy."

"Ah." Professor Osborn's gaze wavered. "George Paulson is your brother?"

Phillip brought a hand to his forehead, wishing his hair was pulled back off his face. He'd not mention the embarrassing barbering inflicted upon his person earlier that day. "Forgive me, sir, I was with the horses and dressed in work clothes when you arrived to deliver Johnny to school. You may not have recognized me."

"Yes, yes, the fellow with the fine bay mare."

"Yes sir, she's a beauty. One of many I've loaned to the school." He didn't need to add that second sentence. But how many times had he spoken with someone and as soon as they'd ascertained he was not the firstborn Paulson son, he was dismissed as being of any consequence.

"Indeed. Are you not the elder brother?"

"No, I'm his younger brother and I manage my father's equestrian interests and teach some at the school."

"I see." His expression revealed doubt. "Most unusual. I'm sure your brother said something…but it's of no matter. You say you're the son who has the fine collection of horses and now you are helping the academy lads?"

"Your youngest son is a fine rider."

"All of my children are." His direct gaze issued a challenge.

All? Including his daughter? "I can see he's had excellent instruction."

"Yes, my eldest son is a fine rider and ensures John is adequately trained."

Johnny had said his sister taught him. The boy hadn't budged from his story even when other boys taunted him and called him a liar. Luckily, fisticuffs had been avoided when the headmaster had wandered along.

"I hate to be presumptuous sir, but I've come to express some concerns to you, in person."

Stroking his bushy salt and pepper moustache, the professor leaned forward. "About his riding?"

"Not at all."

"Do tell." He pointed to a black Windsor chair, seated across from the desk.

Fifteen minutes later, Phillip emerged from the office, spirits sinking. How a man could be cowed by his wife into leaving such a young boy away from home was beyond him. At least Professor Osborne had admitted that his daughter agreed with Phillip's contention that a child so young would be better off with family—especially with his mother and other sister gone off to England.

Phillip trod down the narrow hallway, candlelight flickering from the sconces that lined the corridor and illuminated the wallpaper's intricate pattern. Mrs. Letitia Osborne was surely trying to keep up appearances, but why imitate court fashion here in America? As he reentered the main salon, he spied Martha cornered by Tarleton, again. Gone was her flirtatious manner. Was this her beau? Had he misconstrued their encounter in the chapel? Was he calling her on the carpet for her behavior? Easing through the crush of partygoers clustered around the punch table, he headed to the stables. Uncle Lightfoot might be surprised by his early arrival, but there would no doubt be a lively game of whist ahead for them that night.

Still, he took one last look at the professor's daughter before he headed to the door. Was it his imagination, or did Martha appear angry—and frightened? But then, just as quickly, her demeanor changed altogether. In disgust, he watched as she outright flirted with the man whom he knew to be an ultimate cad. Phillip strode out of the Osborne's home. *What a fool I am.*

She'd been pleasant. Had bitten her tongue at all the inane comments from her brother's young friends, but now with Graham cornering her in the salon, the evening's strain finally caught up with her.

Graham lifted a curl from her cheek and she slapped his hand away. "What are you doing?"

He laughed. "Just admiring what a beauty you are. I always thought so—if only you'd dress to your station and act the part of the lady you are."

Scowling at him, she tried pushing his shoulder to move past, but he didn't budge. "Let me by, Graham."

"Why? We're just getting reacquainted."

"Reacquainted? I've known you a dozen years." She snapped open her fan, tempted to swat him with it.

He leaned in. "I'd hoped you were going to tell me you're going to wager on me and not your brother."

Perspiration dotted her upper lip. Finally, someone was talking about the event, other than giving only sly innuendoes about it to each other. She must convince her brother's former friend that she was, had truly become, an altogether feminine creature who'd never dream of attempting what she had planned. Drawing in a slow breath, she batted her eyelashes at him and assumed a coy demeanor. "Why, you sly boy, I'd break my brother's heart."

His dark eyebrows drew in but then lifted as he laughed. "Does he have a heart?"

She drew her clasped hands to mid-chest. "Just as do half of the wonderful young men at this party."

"Though none are nearly as handsome as me." He arched one eyebrow.

Affecting a high-pitched laugh, she leaned forward. "Perhaps not, but more than one seems unconcerned about our difference in age."

"Is that so?" When he eyed seventy-year-old Professor Robinson, he smirked. "I wondered what the old man had to say to you."

Fury burned in her gut. She had to get out of here. Graham positively unnerved her. When Leah Evans passed by, and Graham swiveled to gawk at the beautiful redheaded girl, Martha slipped away and toward the door, desperate for some fresh air.

Outside, she descended the brick stairs, torches glowing in the courtyard leading to the stables. Somewhere, an owl hooted and horses nickered. The scent of camellias carried on the breeze. Had her imagination tricked her earlier? Had she glimpsed the angel from the bakery? Mayhap God was sending her help. Was there another way to get her brother home from school? Was there another way to independently begin living her own life?

Phillip patted the rental mare's back. She was a sturdy creature standing seventeen hands tall. His Uncle Lightfoot owned a rental livery near the docks on the river, and he'd saved this ride for Phillip. And although his businessman uncle asked him why he was attending the party, Phillip hadn't shared the reason. Even Benjamin, the footman, hadn't been able to extract it from him as he'd brushed Phillip's jacket and tidied him up for the event.

The stablehands carried feed and groomed the other horses in the well-kept building. It was almost as large as the academy's stable and sturdily built of brick.

"Have you seen a guest..." Miss Osborne called out to the men, holding a lamp aloft which softly illuminated her red tresses, making them glow like a halo around her sweet face.

The beauty turned and looked directly at him. Her eyes widened and mouth dropped open. "You?"

He cringed at her tone of disappointment. Perhaps some young women did prefer a man with old-fashioned sensibilities.

"Your hair is gone."

Phillip pressed a hand to the back of his bare neck. "I fear I've been scalped."

Her pretty features relaxed as she carefully strode toward him across the straw-strewn floor. "You're real."

"Of course I'm real." Perhaps, as the baker had suggested, the young woman possessed a confused mind. With all that fan language she was either coy or daft.

After hanging her lamp on a nearby hook, she gazed up at him. "Who are you?"

"I'm your brother's friend. I was here to speak with your father." Which was partially true. He'd also wanted to see this beautiful woman again.

"Brother's friend? Then why aren't you inside with them at the party?"

Because I saw you flirting with all the other men. "I'm his instructor at Yorkview."

"Oh...you mean Johnny!" She clutched his forearm. "How is he? I miss him so." Tears glistened in her eyes.

"He misses you, too." Phillip covered her hand with his own, surprised when she didn't draw back. "I'd come to speak to your father about that very matter."

Maternal concern colored her face. "Is something wrong?"

"I think it's not my place to speak my mind to you, Miss Osborne."

"Please. I believe you are supposed to tell me. I believe..." She looked up at him with a mix of awe and clarity in her eyes. "I believe you are the answer to my prayers."

An answer to her prayers? Hadn't Andrée used to say that to him? Something inside him chilled. The woman who was now his sister-in-law had flirted with him at parties, as Martha had done that night, right up to the night his brother proposed to her.

"I hardly think God would make me the answer to anyone's prayers, as I'm good for few things." Such as riding and training horses and perhaps handling a skiff if the need arose. Anytime a young woman had learned his brother was the heir to Paulson Estates she'd lost interest in him. And when he'd finally thought he'd found the right one, the woman who was God's answer for a wife for him, Andrée had only used that relationship to lure his wedding-shy but competitive brother into asking for her hand. The two deserved each other.

"But Johnny...you've come about something important. And for you to call him your friend and not your pupil makes me believe...makes me hope...that you care for him enough to tell me."

Phillip rubbed his chin. Nearby a horse nickered and another replied in return. "Johnny speaks of you often."

"He misses me, doesn't he?"

When he didn't respond, she squeezed his arm.

"Johnny wants to come home to me! That's why you are here."

What an interesting choice of words. Not that Johnny wished to return to the man who'd seemed so nonchalant, almost cavalier, about what Phillip had shared with him.

Taking Miss Osborne's elbow, he directed her outside to where he'd spied a bench. "Sit down and I'll share. But you must swear you shan't tell your father what I've told you."

Seated beside Johnny's handsome teacher, Martha's heart stuttered and halted whenever, in his melodious voice, he shared about Johnny.

"I read to him nightly. Although he says my falsetto isn't quite up to snuff as I'll never make the ladies in the stories sound so sweet as you do, Miss Osborne."

She couldn't help laughing. "I imagine he much prefers your male voices, though, to my attempts to…" She lowered her voice "…reach a baritone."

He chuckled. "Quite perfect."

"Thank you."

"Let me clarify—that would have been quite perfect for a baritone frog." He laughed at his own joke.

Martha's jaw dropped and she was tempted to swat the man as she would Christopher if he'd teased her like that. "I see. Perhaps you'd let me hear your best feminine voice?"

"Ah." He intertwined his long fingers palms upward, flipped them around and then extending his arms outward, stretching as though he might play a piano. "My dear Mr. Nasty, why I do so love…" He drew out the word 'love' in a long, shrill syllable, irritatingly nasal even to his own ears.

She snorted a laugh. "Oh, sorry, that was unladylike of me. But you were so funny sounding!"

"Johnnie says you've decided you can't be a lady and have given up, but what I saw in there tonight indicates his powers of perception require honing."

She clasped her hands together in delight. "I appeared a lady? How wonderful! I was trying so very hard!"

His golden eyebrows rose and lamplight flickered in his eyes. Or was that something else shining there? He leaned in, took her hand, and raised it to his lips. His very warm, very real, and tender lips. Heat shot up her arm and beneath her capped sleeve. This was no angel but a man. One whose very presence both pulled the air from her lungs yet breathed new life back into her.

"Perhaps we shouldn't be out here alone, Miss Osborne. I'm not interested in engaging in fisticuffs with the other men you've invited to meet with you alone."

"What?" Her shoulders stiffened. "Whatever do you mean?"

"Did you not signal, with your fan, to at least three men inside that they should meet you in private?"

"No!" Her hand flew to her mouth.

"I see." He stood and tucked her arm through his and guided her toward the garden. "Then I suggest you don't look over your shoulder at the gentleman now exiting the house."

"What?" As she tried to look, he used his body to block her view as the back door opened and then closed.

"An older gentleman, a young man of about twenty, and a redheaded young man a bit older."

"But, I…"

He laughed, a rich throaty sound that made her smile. The warmth of his jacketed arm, at her side, seeped through her silk gown as they stepped closer to the small garden.

When they sat on the bench, the full moon emerged from behind the clouds, illuminating the golden curls that framed his handsome face.

"I don't even know your name."

"It's Phillip."

"Phillip?"

He squeezed her hand. "And this time of evening I'm most often found telling tall tales to young men at the academy."

"Is that so?" That meant Johnny wasn't being deprived of his favorite activity. She sighed in contentment but her betraying heart kept hammering away, chasing off the peace she'd hoped to find. "What do you teach?"

"Riding."

"Johnny knows how to ride, I..." Martha stopped herself before she said she'd taught him.

He chuckled. "You've taught him well."

He knew. This man knew. Phillip was aware she'd taught her brother to ride and he didn't laugh at her. Rather, warmth infused his affirmation.

"What else do you teach?"

He shrugged. "A little of this a little of that. Usually history because..." He stopped as though he was withholding something.

"No need to be ashamed if you love history, Phillip. I enjoy it myself."

Again he laughed, a sound she could listen to for the rest of her life. They discussed everything from early colonial immigrants to why Bonaparte would never prevail. And before she'd known it, Jessamine was weaving through the garden calling out for her. And the guests had all departed. Save one.

"Might I call on you when I am again in Williamsburg?" Phillip took her hand and drew it to his lips.

Even through the glove, she felt the warmth of his mouth. "Yes."

"Then you have made me a happy man."

A man. Not an angel. And a happy man at that. "Thank you for speaking with me tonight. And for caring for my brother."

He stood and bowed from the waist. "I shan't keep you out here any longer, Miss Osborne. I fear your brother may expect a duel if you don't return to the house posthaste."

Christopher wouldn't be engaging in much, for he lay abed, having suffered a genuine coughing fit earlier in the day. Martha had been supposed to carry out his social obligations. And Father had hidden himself away in his office, shirking his own responsibilities. Guilt gripped her by the elbows as anger shook her shoulders. She should have been picking up the slack for them, as she had for the rest of the family all these years since her mother had died. "Yes, I shall hurry along."

She lowered her head.

"Wait." Phillip placed one finger beneath her chin and lifted, so that she looked up into his eyes, which glittered in the moonlight.

Might he lean in, and press a kiss to her lips? "What?" she whispered.

He took her hand and pressed something into it. Her fan. When had she dropped it?

"May I request a favor?"

She licked her dry lips. "Certainly."

"Please place your fan in a drawer." He leaned in, pressing his forehead against hers, his breath warm against her cheek. "And only bring it out if I am with you. That way I can tuck it back into my pocket if your invitations are extended to anyone other than myself."

Cheeks heating, she didn't step away, but relished the scent of him, leather and something woodsy, and faint remnants of river air.

The crack of wood beneath someone's heel caused them to separate. Phillip swiveled around, placing himself between her and whoever approached.

"Who the devil are you?" the male voice ground out, issuing with it an unmistakable challenge.

Chapter 5

When the young man stepped into the moonlight, his features were a masculine version of Martha's. When he tipped his chin up, there was no doubt this was Johnny Osborne's older brother.

"Christopher! Go back to bed!" Martha rushed past Phillip. "You're sick and you don't need this night air."

"I saw you." Christopher jabbed a finger in Phillip's direction. "I shall have satisfaction, sir!"

Phillip wouldn't have blamed the young man if he'd thrown a punch at him. "My greatest apologies." He placed a hand to his chest and bent his torso in a brief bow.

"He's from Johnny's school and was comforting me, you ninny!" Martha swatted her fan at her brother's arm. "And he didn't steal a kiss, if that is what you think you saw."

Phillip would never steal a kiss but one day soon he hoped there would be reason, and allowance, for such an endeavor.

With a growl, her brother took two steps forward. "Why would she require comfort? Have you distressed her?"

"Christopher, please! He's a teacher here to tell about…"

"Let me explain." Phillip raised his hands in surrender. "I came to persuade your father to allow your brother to return home from the academy."

Just beyond the garden, an owl swooped from one tall Southern pine to another, its flight carrying a soft "whooshing" sound.

"What?" The young man began to cough so violently that Phillip stepped forward to offer a steadying hand, but the younger, and many inches shorter, man waved him away.

"Let's get you upstairs." Martha slipped Christopher's arm over her shoulder and wrapped her arm around his waist. "Back to bed for you."

"This isn't resolved," Christopher hissed over his shoulder.

"I shall make all aright, sir, at the earliest convenience." And how would he set things straight? Yet again, he was mumbling nonsense. When had his mouth acquired its own mind? Could Phillip extend an offer of marriage to Martha, whom he barely knew? Through Johnny's stories he felt he understood her sweet nature, though, and she certainly pleased the eyes.

Christopher nodded as he and Martha trudged away. "You had better, sir!"

"I shall return so that you are satisfied."

"This is absurd!" Martha turned and gazed at him, the whites of her eyes glowing in the moonlight. "Will you two men fight over a quick embrace of comfort?"

Cotton seemed to have stuffed his mouth.

"You, sir, are no angel!" She made a harrumphing noise. "Offering to duel…"

Phillip had no intention of drawing a pistol against Osborne. Jaw dropping open, he watched as this lovely woman, who was beginning to mean so much to him, departed with her brother. Martha was absolutely correct. He was no angel but a flesh and blood man who'd become so entranced with her he would follow her gentle command like a soldier under a benevolent general. Except there was no war in which she might direct him. Unless that war was for her heart.

As Phillip headed through the chill air to the stables he began whistling the tune to "I Leave My Heart With Thee." Never before had he cared for the parlor song, but now he found it very pleasing.

By the time Phillip was awake and had dressed, his Uncle Lightfoot had long departed for the wharves and Aunt was yet abed. He sat alone in their spacious dining chamber, enjoying breakfast and Caribbean coffee sweetened with rich molasses.

The footman opened the doors to the breakfast room. "The surgeon here to see you, Mr. Paulson."

Phillip pushed back from the long, cherrywood table and stood. "Stephen! Good to see you, my old friend."

Instead of a smile, a tight line kept the doctor's mouth in check until the servant closed the twin doors behind him. "I'm not here about your cousin. I have it on good word from Norfolk that Miranda is fine."

Phillip pointed to the elaborate shield-back chair across from him. "Have a seat."

"I can't stay. I just wanted…" Clutching his hat in one hand, he shoved the other back through his thick sandy hair. "I wondered how George is doing."

"George?" The two men barely knew one another.

"Andrée keeps him on a tight leash, but George knew what he was getting into."

Stephen's eyes locked on his. "Didn't she, now? Still, it's a shame." Sorrow tinged his even features.

"What's a shame?" The two hadn't been able to conceive. That must be what this conversation was about and definitely not something Phillip needed to discuss.

His friend's broad hands shot up defensively, as they had at school when Stephen didn't care to answer a question.

Phillip waved his hand through the air as though dismissing the previous question. "You should come ride with me. It's been too long.

A tentative smile tugged to life on the physician's face. "I'd like that. I've been encouraged by your father to spend a little more time in the saddle."

"My father?" When did those two last see one another?

"Yes. Perhaps I should indeed sit for a moment." Stephen twisted the hat. "I'm forming a men's club you may be interested in joining."

"Oh?"

"Yes, and I've been tasked to approach our peers."

"Men of their late twenties and early thirties?"

Stephen pulled back the heavy chair adjacent to where Phillip sat. After he pushed aside his coat tails, he sat, his light eyes hooded. "Surely even you must understand the need for preparation. For eventualities…"

Unlike his peers, Phillip didn't enjoy hearing tales of war nor did he enter into bombastic arguments about the British and how they believed America was yet their colony. His father and his many friends yet bore the scars and results of that war. He drew in a deep breath, thinking of the boys at Yorkview academy. Who would protect them should war erupt?

He clenched his fists. "Tell me."

Many hours and a boat journey later, Phillip arrived at the wharf of his palatial manor-style home—an imitation of Uncle Dodd's manor home in Gloucester. But unlike Uncle Dodd's abode, across the York River, the servants had not been enslaved. Nor were their workers brought across the ocean on filthy deathtraps that often arrived with less than the "passengers" alive. Instead, Father had hired freedmen and women from across the Commonwealth to work for him.

Phillip mounted the front stairs two at a time and entered the three story columned house. He continued to the dark alcove outside the double doors that opened into the dining room. The brackish scent of the river clung to Phillip's jacket. He'd have it aired and brushed before school on the morrow.

"Massah Phillip, you goin' inside?" Malachi slipped beside him so silently that Phillip jumped. "Sorry, sir, didden mean to startle you."

There must be plantation owners within, visiting with Father, for Malachi to address Phillip as master. "Any reason I shouldn't?"

"They all havin' a meetin', sir."

"Who?"

"Too many to name, sir."

Suddenly, from within, male voices rose, singing the tune of that debauched song "The Anachreon." It was the men's society. All had been together during the war. He strained to hear the words, which his father and his cronies had adapted during the Revolution to reflect their own fight. They'd turned the London gent's drinking song into something inspiring with the new lyrics.

A chill worked its way down his bare neck and to the base of his spine. His friend Stephen had cautioned him, encouraging Phillip to begin a riding club, the young bucks of Williamsburg were going to have their own racing event, and now his father's cronies were gathered in a meeting. And so many young men disappearing from the shores of the Commonwealth. Not only Virginia, but many states along the coast. All seemed connected and Stephen's intimation that peace in their lifetimes might be ending soon sent a chill through him that coursed up his entire body.

Nausea rose up in him. Father and his friends had already seen war in their lifetimes. *Please, Lord... Yet, Thy will be done and prepare me.* Those boys. Martha and her family. They must be protected if Stephen's and others' fears were true.

As the singing ceased, Phillip nodded at the servant, who opened the door. Brushing a strand of hair from his brow, Phillip took three paces forward. Had he been a visitor, and not son, Malachi would have announced him, but he stood aside and then disappeared into the shadows. Striding forward, past the jutting wall that boxed-in the entrance, Phillip sucked in his breath— encircling the table sat almost every patriarch of the plantation owners along the Tidewater peninsular rivers. His heartbeat ratcheted upward. The one exclusion was Tarleton, a longtime British sympathizer married to a beautiful English woman, daughter of a prominent aristocrat.

This gathering could not bode well. Had there already been an invasion somewhere? His gut clenched. "Gentlemen?"

His father nodded to him, his face grim. His leonine silver hair, swept back into a long queue, gleamed in the light of the full onslaught of a half dozen multi-tiered chandeliers.

"Mason?" Father's friend, Mr. Randolph glared at him.

"It's all right. Perhaps it is time my son understood what we are facing."

Prickles of fear chased up his linen sleeves beneath his waistcoat, but he shook them off and strode toward the chair Father indicated, at the far end of the table. As he passed, each man displayed his own unique gesture of irritation or concern—Carter fussing with his napkin, Tyler pulling at his moustache, and so on. By the time he reached his seat, Phillip's nerves were on razor edge. He'd known these men all his life.

To Father's left sat former governor of Virginia, United States Representative, and American Revolutionary War General Lighthorse Harry Lee.

Phillip had the urge to embrace the man, whom he'd known throughout his childhood, but instead he stood stiffly. "Good to see you, General."

"Phillip." Lee nodded, his eyes half-closed.

Compassion coursed through Phillip to see the proud man, brought low and now restored, having recently been released from Debtor's Prison in another county. "Congratulations on your book, sir."

"Thank you."

"Very well written—gave me insight into the war that I didn't get while listening to you and playing with lead soldiers underneath this very table!"

The two older men exchanged an amused glance and lifted their goblets of wine to their lips.

Other men around them continued in conversations. Phillip overheard the words *horses* and *river* as well as profane references to the British.

He ran his tongue over his dry lips.

"Have you come all the way from Alexandria, then?" The Carters had given him and his wife, Anne, a new home there.

"No." Lee again looked to Father and back to Phillip. "My wife and I visited with her family in Charles City."

To Father's right, Edward Colie, a prominent shipbuilder from Maryland, swiveled around. He pushed his spectacles up on his nose and eyed Phillip with suspicion.

Servants began to stream into the room from the doors on the opposite wall from where he had entered. But before they could remove the remnants of the meal, Father cleared his throat and raised one hand. "Hold on a minute. Although he wasn't invited, my son deserves a meal, too, eh, gentlemen?"

To his surprise, the older men laughed and a few banged approval with their fists, causing the silver to clatter against the china plates and Mother's French crystal goblets to bounce.

"Sit down, Phillip!" Father gestured to the far end of the table, where one seat sat empty.

"Yes, sir." He offered a brief bow to the senior men and then crossed the fine wool carpet, one of mother's favorites from her home in France. He pulled out the heavy Chippendale chair and sat.

A servant slipped in alongside him, removed Phillip's Limoges floral china dinner plate and soon returned with chicken slathered with gravy, a biscuit, greens that had been treated with vinegar if their scent was any clue, and mashed yams.

Keeping his head low, over his plate, Phillip feigned a deep interest in his food and listened as the men resumed their conversations.

"Do you think it's true?" Nearby, Randolph asked Smythe.

"I do. And we're so undermanned it could be over in the wink of an eye if this..." he let out a string of profanity, "government of ours..."

"I agree. And with their Canadian lackeys to the north, who knows how far and how fast things could go with the British?"

"Quite true." Mr. Randolph's craggy features bunched into a frown.

Just beyond Randolph and Smythe sat Mr. Hamilton and Mr. Williams of Charles City's fine plantations and also governor Tyler's brother. First Families of Virginia. Many of these men's sons were premier students at school, the Smythe boy professing, as George once had, that he would be "a man of education, a teacher and not a planter."

"No dessert tonight, Gentlemen, but Mariah has made sweet bread for you to tote home with you." Father stood and waved toward the sideboard.

"Hear! Hear!" Again, the men became rowdy.

Normal conversation resumed, with the servants slipping in to refill cups and carry off dirty dishes. Phillip relaxed slightly, glad no imminent danger was discussed. For surely they'd have torn into that topic posthaste, had there been.

He leaned back in his chair. The fifteen foot long Chippendale table, its soiled linen tablecloth now removed, seemed to stretch forever, but in actuality seated only twenty, and every seat was occupied. Where was George? Why wasn't he there? Stephen's words, spoken as a physician, hinted that something other than fatherhood was amiss with George. For a moment, with the men's jovial voices still ringing, it almost seemed as though the former soldiers were in an encampment of sorts. Taking a quick tally, he counted a dozen who'd served during the Revolution and his heart began to hammer. *They do truly fear an invasion.* This was why Stephen hemmed and hawed and discussed horses at such great length, and why men needed to retain a good seat and horsemanship skills, and why they must rouse up a good club of riders.

He pushed his seat back as the other men began to rise and leave. Several shook his hand, and he stood, still a little dazed. No wonder so many militiamen had ensured their mounts were the very best.

"Got a one-year-old for my younger brother, Phillip?" Mr. Williams leaned in and shook Phillip's hand.

"Every yearling but one has already been earmarked for an owner. And won't be sent off until they are fully trained, which is closer to two."

Williams leaned in and whispered, "My brother wishes to meet you tomorrow at the Heron."

"The Nesting Heron?" Phillip arched an eyebrow at the man. "You jest."

"No, I do not." Williams pushed free from the table and stood.

"He's rather young to be in such rough company as he'll find at the Heron."

The plantation owner waved at Phillip dismissively. "Don't disappoint him. He'll be accompanied by some friends whom your father will discuss with you. We need your help."

Sweat trickled down Phillip's brow and he wiped it away with the back of his hand. "I'll see what I can do." He unkinked his frame and stood to his full height.

Narrowing his eyes, Williams looked up at him. "We see a great many gentlemen from Washington City gathering at our home in Charles City, and we are now of one accord. Carter will apprise you of our plans."

Phillip nodded curtly and Williams returned the gesture then turned to leave.

The rest of the gentlemen streamed from the room, the older former militiamen clapping their hands on Father's shoulder as they went.

Only Lee remained and Hamilton. A chill moved through Phillip again. The Williams family had access to many ships as did Colie. The British could arrive only by sea.

"Would you join us, Son?" Father tapped his pocket—the telltale sign he was hoping to smoke his pipe soon. "We've much we wish to share with you."

How could it be that just as he was on the verge of spending more time with a woman who could convert any house into a home, Phillip now must consider the prospects his old friend warned of? Horses and war. And here he'd considered his livelihood a peaceful countryside existence. No more.

Chapter 6

In the distance, beneath thick-as-pudding clouds that hovered over Queen's Creek inlet, Uncle Lightfoot's dock loomed. At least with the mandatory visit with young Williams, Phillip had been able to use this as the excuse he needed to return to Williamsburg and bring the little Osborne boy for a visit.

Johnny squeezed Phillip's hand. "Are we almost home?"

An arrow of pity pierced his heart. "Remember what I cautioned, for you shall not remain at home."

The child's full lower lip quivered and a tear trickled down his pale cheek. He sniffed and pushed back a stray strand of hair. "Yes, sir."

On impulse, Phillip bent and lifted the boy up into his arms, surprised at how light he was—definitely not the sturdy little fellow who'd been deposited with them several months earlier. With one hand he clutched the rail and the other he held the boy to his chest. What would it be like to have his own children? A child with reddish hair like his mother's? He'd not been able to keep an image of Martha from flashing in his mind. Who was he fooling? He wasn't bringing the child here simply to assuage her concerns. Nor to dissuade her from any aspirations of racing with those young men whose exercise was in reality the beginning of training for possible future invasion by the British. No, he was here for a much more selfish reason. He, like this boy, needed to see her again. To see her light green eyes fixed upon his own.

"Do you think she could tell me a story before I go?"

The schooner shifted suddenly and Phillip held tight, flexing his knees as the crew began the process of securing them to the dock. Mates called out and a horn sounded. When silence, save for the lapping of the water, resumed, he set Johnny down. "I imagine she might."

"Marty's stories are almost as good as yours."

"Marty?"

"That's what I call her."

"I see. I used to call my brother..." He caught himself before revealing his brother's nickname. It wouldn't do for the boy to slip and refer to his headmaster as Old Sneezy.

A gray-haired man ran up the docks, his muscular form leaving no doubt that this was Jefferson Lightfoot.

"Uncle!" Phillip waved.

"Who've you got with you, lad?" His uncle shaded his eyes and squinted at Johnny.

Mussing the boy's wavy hair, Phillip called out, "One of Williamsburg's brightest young scholars!"

The child gazed up at him, blinking. "Am I?"

"Of course. Or you wouldn't be at our academy."

The six–year-old straightened his shoulders and stood taller, as the crew set the plank down for them to climb down.

"Need to speak with you, Nephew!" From below, Phillip's uncle scowled up.

Soon they had disembarked and joined Uncle Lightfoot on the wharf. He handed Johnny a coin and pointed to a cart piled with buns. "Go get one, Son."

"Thank you, sir!"

As the child ran off, Phillip extended his hand. "How are you and Auntie?"

"Good, good." As usual, his uncle delivered his bone-crunching grip and Phillip fought the urge to wince.

"What did you wish to speak of?"

He passed his broad chapped hand over his wide jawline. "I need to speak of the boy's brother—Christopher."

Phillip stiffened as his relative's harsh tone. "What is it?"

"I don't trust those other young men racing against him."

He exhaled a loud breath. "I feel the same, sir."

"Especially with rumors about his mother."

"Agreed." His father and his cronies had explained who, and what, they believed Letitia Osborne to truly be. And if the boy's mother was a British spy, as they believed, the entire family may be in danger.

Johnny paid the proprietor of the cart and was racing back toward them, happily munching on his bun.

Uncle leaned in. "Also, I know some things even your father isn't privy to. Please make plans to stay the evening."

"I cannot tonight, sir, but perhaps in a fortnight."

"No, you must take time this evening. I will send word."

"I..." He'd finish this argument later, when they returned. Phillip had obligations to keep at Yorkview Academy even if Father and Uncle both thought they could commandeer his time.

A woman's voice faintly carried on the breeze. From beyond the wharf, a figure, cloaked in a pale muslin day dress, hurried toward the docks, long pink ribbons from her straw hat bouncing against her lacy shawl-covered chest. *Martha.*

Johnny spun and ran to her and threw himself into his sister's arms.

A lump formed in Phillip's throat and a bit of river spray seemed to have found his eyes.

Uncle swiveled to follow Phillip's gaze and then turned back to grin up at him. "Taken a fancy to a certain young lady, I see?"

Before Phillip could protest, his uncle laughed and squeezed his arm. "Bring her to dinner. I'd welcome an opportunity to know Letitia's stepdaughter better. And you'd best learn what she knows, as well."

His conspiratorial tone sped a chill up Phillip's jacketed arm as the man released his grip. If Martha Osborne did know...what then?

Looking at the beautiful young woman as she embraced her brother, he couldn't imagine her being anything other than goodness and light—and the lady he wished to know much better. Just not in the way his uncle implied.

Since she'd received the message from the Lightfoots that Phillip *Paulson* should be arriving that day, Martha had worried herself silly. First was the realization that he was a member of one of the wealthiest families in the Commonwealth. Why did he convey the impression that he was Johnny's instructor, then? But he'd never actually mentioned his surname and she'd not asked.

Jessamine had come up from the kitchen to help arrange Martha's hair. "You gotta let me fix that mess of yours, Miss Martha."

With all the tossing and turning she'd done the night before, dreaming of her angel—no, Phillip Paulson—her red hair poufed out in all directions. "Yes, please."

Now, after a full hour of brushing and combing, her tresses were more elaborate. "Thank you, Jessamine."

"You welcome. You gonna need help dressing today." The servant assisted Martha into one of her prettier gowns and affixed Mother's gold and garnet broach to her ecru lace shawl.

Martha peered into her mirror. She almost looked like a gentlewoman.

Jessamine cocked her head. "What time you say he comin'? It nigh on the hour, Missy."

Gasping, Martha grabbed her reticule from her dressing table. "I've got to go."

"Already told Asa to get the carriage ready."

"Bless you." Martha exhaled a sigh as she departed.

Within a short while, Asa stopped at the docks, despite the driver's protest that it was "no place for a lady." But she couldn't wait for Phillip's arrival with Johnny.

Her heart pounded as she disembarked. Why was Phillip returning so soon? She'd thought little of anything else since he'd departed.

Now many hours later, Martha sighed in contentment at the end of the whirlwind day. She and Phillip had discussed everything from Aristotle to the best hunting dogs to their favorite parlor songs. Meanwhile, Johnny visited with Father, Christopher, and the one little boy on their lane who was allowed to play with her younger brother.

She had to tell him, had to get Phillip to promise to have Johnny sent home. So as they sat in the Market Square, in the center of Williamsburg, Martha told him all about her plans to race with Christopher's friends to Yorktown, taking his place.

Phillip quirked a golden eyebrow. "Did you know I am an entrant?"

"No."

He reached into his coat pocket and pulled out the map that she'd found in Christopher's bedchamber. "See?"

She puffed out a breath. "If I win, which I shall, then I can use the money to purchase that small stable on the other end of town."

His eyes widened. "To what purpose?"

"I shall live there out from beneath Letitia's critical eye."

"Is she so harsh as all that?"

"Worse than you can imagine."

His handsome features tugged as though he was holding something back. "What if she never returns?"

She stiffened. "My stepmother has always come back before."

Phillip swiveled away from her, shielding his eyes from the sun and peering in Johnny's direction. "I don't see how anyone could leave Johnny behind. Surely she'd return for him…"

Unease trickled through her as clouds dimmed the autumn sun's warmth. "When she comes back I'll be in the little house beside the stable and Johnny can visit me any time he wishes."

Phillip turned toward her, his countenance unreadable as he scanned her face as though searching for something. "When do you expect her?"

Martha shrugged. "We've had no word, but she's often gone for over half the year and it's only now a few months."

"Is your father not concerned that he's had no communication?"

Again she shrugged. "We don't discuss it. And I don't wish to upset him by bringing it up."

"Understandable." A smile tugged at his mouth. "Back to our previous topic; you expect to race those young bucks and win?"

"Of course! I'm better than any of them."

"I think not."

Her only true competitor was Graham and if he was any kind of gentleman, once he determined it was she, not her brother racing, he'd let her win. At least that was her hope. "It's true whether you choose to believe it or not."

"I'll wager there is one man who could best you."

"And if he does not?"

"I shall move heaven and earth to get Johnny home to you, regardless of what that may do to my relationship with my brother and your father."

"You would?"

"Yes."

Martha clapped her hands together. "Thank you, Lord."

"You might thank me also." Phillip stroked his strong jawline.

"Thank you, Phillip."

"And if you do not beat that other equestrian, then Johnny goes where I say, including staying at school."

"Agreed." Martha narrowed her eyes at him as a breeze swirled leaves around them.

He removed his watch from his vest pocket and frowned. "We must leave soon." Phillip took her hand in his, sending a thrill through her.

She sighed. "I know."

"Might I presume that since you accepted me as an Academy instructor, that you'd permit me to court you even though I am the second son?"

There was an urgency in his voice that Martha hadn't heard before. "How could I refuse the man who brought my little brother to me?"

He laughed. "So that was all I had to do?"

She arched an eyebrow at him. "Not if you were trying to get Father's permission." She sighed.

"He did seem a tad angry, didn't he?"

"Yes, but I don't think Johnny noticed."

"No."

Johnny raced through the thick amber, orange, and red leaves in the market square, chasing a squirrel and laughing. Myrtle James had given the child several cookies which Johnny consumed on the spot; likely fueling the energy he displayed that afternoon.

"Think he's had enough?" Phillip glanced between her and the carriage, parked near the hatmakers, where she'd purchased a new brown tricornered felt cap for her brother.

"Between skipping rocks on the pond, riding his pony at home, and dining at Mrs. Grunst's fine tavern, I believe the boy is about to collapse."

As if to demonstrate her words, Johnny tossed his new cap in the air, fell onto his back in the leaves, and his hat twirled in the air before landing atop his slim form. A gray squirrel snatched up an acorn nearby and ran off.

Phillip laughed. "I'd say he's ready."

"Well past exhaustion but perfectly pleased!" She squeezed Phillip's hand.

He swiveled to face her and lifted her fingers to his lips and kissed them, spiraling heat through her. Martha sucked in her breath and he lowered her arm, then took one step closer to her, leaning his forehead down. Was he going to kiss her? She blinked, unsure if she should close her eyes.

Nearby, several servants giggled as they walked past. When she went to draw back, Phillip cupped her chin in his palm and gazed intently into her eyes.

"Do you wish to be courted by me, Miss Osborne?"

"Yes." She closed her eyes and waited for his mouth to cover her own. Hadn't he just asked permission to kiss her? Warm lips pressed against her forehead.

"I assume that is your answer, my dear." His chest rumbled with laughter as he pulled her into a brief embrace and then stood back.

Embarrassed, she ducked her chin, but his gentle fingers cupped her there and lifted her face. Looking into those beguiling eyes she couldn't utter a word. He really did look too handsome to be real. But he was. And he wished to court her. Martha Osborne, the outcast of Williamsburg.

"I must go soon, as I have another engagement." His eyelids dropped to half-mast and his lips twitched in distaste.

Another engagement? Of what did he speak? Phillip had mentioned nothing prior to now.

"I should go home."

"Nonsense. I'll have one of my uncle's drivers carry you back. You'll be able to spend more time with Johnny, then."

Phillip mentioned nothing of wishing to spend more time with her. Was he toying with her affections? Her shoulders stiffened. But she'd go— she'd get to say goodbye to Johnny. "As you wish."

His features relaxed again. Phillip tilted back his head, chuckled, and released her hands. "As you wish! My mother said if a woman ever said those words to me, and meant them, that I'd have found my own true love."

"Is that so?"

"Yes. She loved a parlor song about such a silly notion. Used to have George and I practice it on the piano forte."

Martha tilted her head. "I did mean my words but please don't play that dreadful tune..." She'd been about to say *when we are married* but caught herself. Perhaps there would be no wedding if he was meeting with other young women.

"As you wish." He winked at her and bowed before striding off toward Johnny.

Johnny ran back, then threw his arms around her waist. "I don't want to leave you, Marty."

A muscle near Martha's eye twitched and she drew in a slow breath. "You'll be home soon." If she had anything to say about it. Plus, if she won her wager then Phillip would assist her with bringing Johnny back to Williamsburg.

A buckskin-clad lone rider directed his sorrel toward them, dismounting in one fell swoop when he neared the hitching post. The horse's coat gleamed, its reddish hue almost the exact shade of her own hair. Despite the backwoodsman's rough appearance, his mount had been well-tended.

"Paulson! I have a message for you." As the man strode toward them, he retrieved a missive from a fringed deerskin pouch hung from his neck. "Believe your meeting time has changed."

Chapter 7

Surely if Phillip was meeting a lady she'd not send message in such a manner. Martha resisted the urge to peer over Phillip's shoulder.

Phillip tore into the note and grinned. "Thanks, Shad. Let the men know I got their message."

The knot that had formed in Martha's stomach suddenly released.

"Sure thing, Paulson." The rider tipped his hat at Martha then departed.

His smile broad, Phillip clapped his hands together. "Off to the wharf!"

When they arrived, the sun was sitting low on the horizon. Martha hugged Johnny close to her before removing the light wool blanket that covered their laps in the open carriage. After Phillip set the brake, one of the Lightfoot's servants ran from the stable and assisted him out.

Martha stepped down into Phillip's outstretched arms. He held her there more than was proper, his arms warm and strong at her waist.

I am being courted by him! Her heart sped up as he pressed another kiss to her forehead. How long would it be until she saw him once more? It wouldn't be proper to ask.

From behind her, Johnny jumped out, landing with a thud.

She laughed, "Some things never change. You're a little taller, Johnny, and still full of energy."

A cloud seemed to pass over Phillip's eyes. "He's a stalwart chap and will need that stamina."

What a strange thing to say. But then again, didn't all boys need energy and strength?

Mr. Lightfoot strode out from his office, a drab wooden structure at the edge of the wharf. His eyes took her and Johnny in before his silver head tipped back and he surveyed the darkening sky.

Phillip rubbed his chin. "Seems the tides and the wind align against my return this evening."

Glancing to the creek, it was clear the tide had already departed—without Phillip.

"I see." Hope lifted, like a breeze from the water, which was calm as a looking glass.

Johnny propelled himself at Phillip. "Can we stay?"

Mr. Lightfoot joined them, rubbing his beefy hands together, a grin forming on his ruddy face.

"Perhaps this might be the night to dine with my Uncle Lightfoot?" Phillip arched an eyebrow at the older man.

"You must have gotten the message, then?"

"I did." The two exchanged glances and a shadow once again passed over Phillip's features.

What did those men want to meet with him about?

Mr. Lightfoot patted his mid-section. "I say we have our dinner sooner rather than later."

The dimming sun illuminated the faint blond bristle on Phillip's cheeks. On his very handsome face. He rubbed his jaw, as though aware of her thoughts. "We have to get word to Professor Osborne immediately."

Martha nodded. "Yes, he may wish him to return home."

"Is your father a practical man, Miss Osborne?"

"Indeed."

"Then best to send word you and your brother shall remain for dinner as well as the evening, for he and Phillip would go out on the tide first thing."

"Yes, sir."

"Your brother is most welcome at the children's table where he may make as much noise as he wishes."

Johnny let out a whoop.

"Perhaps not that kind of noise at dinner, Johnny." Phillip leaned down.

He took her hand. "And we shall send you home by a coachlit carriage, my dear."

His dear? Those words sent a tremor through her. They weren't uttered the way Father's friends had, when they had referred to Martha as "my dear."

"You must be shaved and readied for dinner, Nephew. You're covered with dust." Lightfoot clapped his broad hand against Phillip's back and Martha felt him flinch.

Martha passed her hand over her best day gown's skirt and particles of dust puffed from her as well. She'd retrieved her pelisse from home but it hadn't protected her gown. "I'm not in evening attire."

Mr. Lightfoot waved his hand. "Our maids can brush your clothing out before dinner. Do not worry."

A broad-chested worker rolled barrels down the walkway. "I'll send my worker with a message."

"Perhaps it is best we go." Martha was worn out from people being upset with her, although with Letitia gone she had experienced a reprieve.

"Please, Marty, can we stay?" Johnny squeezed Martha's hand so hard that she flinched and pulled free.

"All right then. I fear you've all convinced me. Thank you, Mr. Lightfoot. But of course, if Father disapproves…"

A pelican, perched on a nearby pole at the dock, peered at them, with much the same expression as Mr. Lightfoot. "I imagine your father will enjoy a glad heart if his children are happy. That is how it is for we fathers, I assure you."

Was it so? Father didn't seem to care how miserable Johnny had been at school. Martha nibbled her lip as Phillip extended his arm. Warmth and strength were offered in his solid forearm as he swiveled her back away from the docks and toward the stables.

"Why don't you have a seat on the bench while I request a carriage? Then we'll ride to Uncle's home." Phillip pointed to a narrow wooden slat, nailed to two squared off stumps which might have once been masts. It nestled near a square, whitewashed building by the dock.

Martha took Johnny's small hand in hers. "Not much of a seat, but it will do."

"As long as I'm with you, Marty!" Her brother snuggled against her.

They both leaned back against the building, the sun's fading rays warm. After the delight of spending the day with her brother, the fear of having him leave again, and now having a reprieve, Martha's emotional reserves were reaching their end. Tears of relief began to trickle down her cheeks. Thankfully, the little fellow didn't look up. She needn't upset him. Somehow she'd discreetly fish out her handkerchief with her right hand and gently dab at her cheeks without disturbing him.

Gentle, even breathing, suddenly accompanied by a low snore announced that the day's events had taken a toll on Johnny, too.

Quiet movement to her right, and then a handkerchief extended to her, once again cued her to not only Phillip's presence, but also his ability to anticipate her needs.

"Thank you," she mouthed.

He briefly raised his eyebrows in acknowledgement and then pointed to a nearby stable.

In a short while, the two men returned, in a fine black carriage, the Lightfoot crest painted on the side in gold and red. Martha's breath caught in her chest. Brass lights were affixed on the sides of the carriage and in the front. It would be dark later when they returned home and the lights would be necessary.

Soon, Phillip carried Johnny to the brougham as Mr. Lightfoot offered his arm, which felt surprisingly sinewy beneath his blue broadcloth coat. "Very glad to entertain you this evening, Miss Osborne."

"Thank you, sir."

"I'm an old friend of your mother's, you know."

She almost tripped over some pebbles beneath the crushed oyster shell path as they headed to the carriage. "No, I didn't know."

He stopped, and faced her. "I apologize that I haven't been the friend to your father that he needed. And someone you could have turned to, my dear."

Before she could respond, Phillip returned and assisted her up into the interior. She sucked in a breath. She slid onto the brown leather seat and ran a hand over its smooth surface. Crimson velvet lined the interior and the ceiling was quilted, with large fabric-covered buttons affixed in each diamond corner of the pattern.

Johnny lay rolled on his side. After rearranging his legs, she sat next to her brother. Mr. Lightfoot entered the coach and sat opposite, with Phillip following.

Mr. Lightfoot rapped on the ceiling and called out, "Move on!"

Johnny's head jerked up. He eyed Martha lazily, but then dropped his head again.

The carriage suddenly heaved forward. She'd have lost her balance had Phillip not reached across and pressed a hand to her knee. She clutched

Johnny to prevent him from rolling off the slippery, leather cushioned seat and Phillip splayed a steadying hand over her brother's bent knees. She cringed, expecting either him or his uncle to launch into a string of profanity at the driver, as so many men might do.

Mr. Lightfoot shook his silvery head while a muscle jumped in Phillip's cheek and a tendon in his neck protruded against his stiff white cravat.

"I assure you there was no need to change, my dear." Mrs. Lightfoot, who smelled of roses and sugar cookies, took Martha's hands in her slim ones. The petite woman blinked rapidly and then flipped Martha's hands over, revealing stray callouses from the reins.

Martha pulled her hands free. "I'm afraid I…"

"…ride like a banshee, like your mother used to do?" The pretty matron tipped her head back and laughed. "No one could hunt like she could."

"And you, did you join them, too?"

"Oh yes, indeed—but that was a long time ago, before I had children." Mrs. Lightfoot's eyes glimmered beneath her ruffled cap. "If only I'd had the gift of riding that my nephew has, though."

"Oh." Which nephew did she mean?

"Phillip is the premier horseman in all of Virginia. Some say the entire land."

"What?" And he was going to ride in the race. And he was the equestrian he'd referred to. She tried to recall what he'd said when they'd made their wager.

Phillip, clean-shaven, entered the room attired in his same clothing but brushed clean.

The tiny woman rose and rearranged the skirt of her striped gown. "I was just telling Miss Osborne what an accomplished rider you are. I thought everyone knew."

"Only those who've ridden with me," he said dryly, "and been left in my dust."

Martha coughed. "Is that so?"

"Indeed."

Ginger colored curls bobbed beneath Mrs. Lightfoot's cap as she nodded in agreement.

The savory scent of ham carried into the parlor.

Phillip extended his hand to Martha. "Uncle says his invitation still stands and we shall have a formal dinner in a fortnight—crystal, china, and all."

In a fortnight, she'd have won the race, had her brother home, and not have to put up with nonsense about her brother being better off at the academy. For surely Phillip wouldn't deliberately win, would he? He'd not have made that offer knowing she'd never beat him in the race, would he?

Mrs. Lightfoot called over her shoulder, "But tonight we shall eat family style." Then she exited the parlor, leaving Phillip and Martha momentarily alone.

She tentatively accepted his hand and stood. "I hope the dining chairs aren't as uncomfortable as this tiny wooden chair." The embroidered cushion, on which she'd just sat, was ineffectual. Was her plan to join the race just as ridiculous?

From somewhere in the large house, the laughter of children carried.

"I should have told you of my prowess, Martha, but I feared I would sound like a braggart."

"Yet you allowed me to make such a claim!" She released his hand and crossed her arms over her chest.

"I had my reasons."

Martha tried to tamp down her irritation. "Such as?"

"What if leaving Johnny at the academy is a safer…a better alternative?"

Safer? Better? She resisted the urge to snort out her rebuke. Instead, she drew in a slow breath. "Since I cannot imagine that ever being the case, I can't even remark." She smiled up at him in what she wished was a charming manner, although she felt anything but at the moment.

He ran his thumb over his lower lip. "There may be situations. Events. That might change your mind."

Infuriated, she squeezed her hands until her fingernails dug into her palms. She must speak with Phillip and bring him back around to her way of thinking. And she mustn't let him distract her from preparing for the race and from anticipating that she would indeed win.

Mr. Lightfoot's silver head appeared in the parlor doorway as he peeked in. "Come along now or we'll be eating cold food like I had to endure in the army."

His wife ducked her head beneath her husband's arm and rolled her blue eyes. "In the army. In the army. I imagine we shall be regaled with tales of all your deprivations, again, since we have a new guest."

Laughing heartily, he turned, took his wife's arm, and steered her out the door, calling over his shoulder, "The children are already seated."

Phillip closed the distance between them and offered his hand. "We shan't have anything to eat if my cousins take a first crack at dinner."

Although she wanted to remain angry with him, Martha couldn't help smiling.

But by the end of the evening, Martha's nerves were frayed. Was it her imagination, or did both Mr. and Mrs. Lightfoot inquire just a little too much about Letitia? Stepmother was a beautiful woman and while Martha didn't want to believe the recent rumors that she may have a lover in England, something about their questions, as well as Phillip's earlier ones, made her suspect there could be truth in the suspicion. Had Letitia also kept paramours in Williamsburg? Surely not beneath her father's nose.

Chapter 8

The fragrant spicy scent of pumpkin soup carried as Dicey entered the parlor where Martha was doing handwork near the window. The servant deftly pressed down the top of the tilt-top cherrywood parlor table, secured the latch, and set a cup atop the shiny surface. "You got to eat, Miss Martha."

"I know." But how could she when she'd received no word from Phillip in a week? Had her worst fears proved true? Was he simply playing with her heart?

"Thank you, Dicey."

"Yes'm. Now you eat up."

After she set her tatting aside, Martha forced herself to taste a spoonful. Delightful. But not nearly as wonderful as it would be to view Phillip's handsome face across the table. She'd risk breaking her teeth and eat a dozen of Mrs. Lightfoot's tasteless rolls if only she could sup with Phillip. She sighed, pushed the cup away, and lifted the tatted star she'd begun.

When Mother was alive, the two of them would work together and create stars to give to friends at Christmas. Would Martha ever marry and have the chance to pass on this tradition? After wiping a tear away, she resumed her work, soon lost in memories of the many years she'd sat in this parlor with her loving mother.

The clock chimed the hour and Martha looked up from her cushioned chair, sensing someone watching.

Graham Tarleton leaned lazily against the doorframe of the Osborne's parlor. "All alone, are we?"

Martha startled, and dropped her work. "No. Father is in his study."

"Ah, just as well, for Lady Mother invites you for tea—now, if you are able."

Martha couldn't exactly say she was unable as she was dressed.

He arched an eyebrow "Your brother, too—if he's up to it."

Had he just referred to Christopher as her brother, and not as Chris, his pet name? Perhaps the two had not overcome their disagreement, after all.

How slack his body seemed compared to the taught energy in Phillip's. How disingenuous Graham's smile in comparison with the teacher's easy grin. Yet Phillip wished to now keep her brother from her. Wasn't that what he implied by saying Johnny might be safer there? Martha clenched her fists.

Her father joined them. "Good to see you, Graham."

He clapped Graham on the shoulder and offered his hand. The two men shook. "Good to see you, Professor."

Was Father oblivious to the rift that had borne out between Christopher and Graham? Was his mind so cluttered by the detritus of his philosophical ponderings that he truly didn't notice the emotional status of his children?

A sad, sickening truth landed in the pit of her stomach. Her father really didn't care. Not in the paternal way he should. Not in love and protection. Not like Phillip seemed to do. But hadn't her beau, if he was indeed that, now changed his tune and wanted to keep Johnny from home?

"Martha, you should take Graham up on his mother's offer. Would do you a world of good to get out in polite society for a change."

"And you are not polite society, sir?" Graham laughed, but her father only stared at him blankly for a minute.

Then dawning of understanding showed on Father's face. "Well, you know how it is when the men outnumber the women in a house, don't you?"

"Indeed, I do sir. With my sisters married, my mother seems desperate for me to bring another young woman into our household." He grinned at Martha. "Perhaps a wife and another daughter for her to spoil, as she did my sisters."

Spoiled they were, for no two more rotten young women had Martha ever met. As far as a wife for Graham, she would never be that woman. Still, she was so perturbed with both Phillip and her father that she could use a change of pace. "Let me at least help ease part of your mother's distress by giving her company."

Graham bowed at the waist.

She couldn't help adding, "By providing female companionship, mayhap I'll relieve you of your perceived obligation to thrust a new daughter-in-law upon your mother."

Her stepmother and Mrs. Tarleton had been very close friends, both being daughters of British descent and married to much older husbands. The two reminded her of twin Siamese cats for some reason. She could almost sense claws crawling up her spine and she shivered.

A spicy scent permeated the air in the Osborne's vestibule, clashing with the warmth of the October day. Phillip stood, clutching his hat, awaiting the servant's return.

Professor Osborne emerged from a nearby doorway and strode toward him. "Mr. Paulson?"

"Johnny is quite well, sir." Phillip straightened his shoulders, straining the fabric of his greatcoat. "I've come to see your daughter."

"Very good about Johnny." He scratched his jaw. "But I fear Martha is out."

Nearby, a female servant passed, casting a furtive glance their way.

"Do you know when she'll return?"

"She's gone to the Tarleton's home. Likely not back for many hours, since Mrs. Tarleton takes elaborate teas."

"I see." The Tarleton's imposing home was situated many blocks away. "I shan't keep you then, sir. Thank you."

Once outside, Phillip pulled his pocket watch from his vest pocket. He drew in a lungful of air saturated with moisture. The skies portended a downpour if he was correct. As though in answer, three fat raindrops fell in succession on his nose. He lowered his head and barreled on to where he'd left his conveyance and horse. He would see Martha. He had to. Even if that meant they risked getting rained on in the open carriage.

Finally, he arrived at the Tarleton's Georgian brick manor. The bitter scent of recently trimmed boxwoods assaulted his nose. He hurried up the steps to a small porch over which hung an oval portico. A warm gust of wind blew the rain at him as the door opened and a coffee-skinned manservant opened the door. No, not a servant—a slave—for Mrs. Tarleton kept a contingent of them, a bevy for the household and stables, as though she were still a noblewoman in Britain.

The dark-eyed man waved Phillip in and took his hat. Numerous candelabras' flickering lights illuminated the grand foyer, decorated in traditional marble tile. Men's laughter and deep voices echoed from nearby. Mahogany paneling and a pleasant curved stairway, whose walls were dominated by aristocrats' portraits, drew Phillip's attention.

The servant swiveled to face him. "Mr. Tarleton has guests, sir. May I announce you?" The man's diction was proper high class British. Phillip blinked at him.

"No, I'm here for Miss Osborne. I believe she's having tea with Mrs. Tarleton?"

"Lady Tarleton, you mean." The rebuke didn't go unnoticed, and Phillip flexed his hands, considering whether he should correct the servant or not. Lady or not, this was America and she held no title here.

"Please tell her that Phillip Paulson is here for Miss Osborne."

Giving him a wary eye, the man removed himself to the nearby parlor.

A portrait at the bottom of the stairs caught his eye. Both the man and the woman looked familiar. Dressed in a British admiralty uniform, a dark-haired man stood next to a beautiful young woman whose auburn tresses were arranged in piles atop her head, a tiara securing the curls in place. Above, and to the left, hung an image of Johnny Osborne, dressed in old-fashioned clothing. Phillip coughed. It wasn't the child, couldn't be—not in the decades-old breeches and tunic he wore, a sash draped across his chest.

From the other room, Mr. Tarleton's voice boomed, "Admiral, you have a wicked sense of humor."

Admiral Pemberley? A British naval officer welcomed at a home in Virginia? "Lady" Tarleton may be the military man's cousin, but in these trying times, was such a visit even allowed? Shouldn't Pemberley be out there chasing after Napoleon? Phillip's skin crawled. He drew in a steadying breath. What had he stumbled upon? And Martha was here, too? Was she conspiring with them?

Another man's voice rumbled something and suddenly Mr. Tarleton appeared in the doorway of a room on the left. "Oh, it's you, Paulson. I fear I have guests and cannot receive you."

"Yes, sir, but I understand my sweetheart is here. Came to retrieve her. Poor thing must have forgotten we had an engagement tonight…" Phillip strained to recall what was being performed but couldn't remember the name, perhaps because he wasn't being quite honest. He hadn't yet even asked Martha. "At the theater."

Confusion flickered over the man's thick features. Then he blinked. "Ah, yes, one of Shakespeare's finest! A fine play. Mrs. Tarleton and I saw it two night's past. But whom is this sweetheart you speak of? Thought all the young ladies abandoned you for George."

Martha eased as far forward in her seat as she could, having overheard Phillip's voice in the hallway. She'd searched for a way to leave ever since she'd arrived to discover that her host had welcomed British naval officers into his home.

"Do try the watercress. It's all the rage in London." Mrs. Tarleton lifted one finger, directing one of her slaves to carry a tray of tiny sandwiches to Martha, and used an elaborately engraved silver serving piece to slide several onto her plate.

"Thank you."

Her hostess arched an eyebrow. "Surely your mother doesn't have you thank your servants, does she?"

Martha bit back her retort that Letitia wasn't her mother. She might as well ask what she was wondering. "Mrs. Tarleton, are those indeed British naval officers I saw with your husband?"

Even Martha knew harboring such persons was terribly inappropriate, if not illegal. So many young men had disappeared along America's coastline, impressed into service with the British navy.

Was Phillip here to sell horses to the British navy? And if so, what did that mean? Bile rose in her throat, but she raised the cup of Bohea tea to her lips and sipped slowly, the steam from the porcelain cup warming her face.

Dear God, have you put me here to allow me to see this? So I can warn others? Please steady my nerves. Who could she tell? Who could she trust? Her brother would know. She must get home, where Christopher rested in bed. Perhaps this information would rouse him enough to get up and make some effort to recover.

The men continued to converse but their words no longer carried. Then she heard Mr. Tarleton's mocking laugh.

"Excuse me." Martha pushed back from the table.

At the senior Tarleton's insult, Phillip's cheeks burned. He'd better depart before his fist could connect with the man's narrow jaw.

What had he seen here? Perhaps rumors were true — the professor's family was in favor of British rule and would support them in the case of invasion.

Martha, wearing a pretty dress that brought out the jade color of her eyes, emerged from a nearby room. "Phillip! What are you doing here?"

He exhaled a puff of air. "To court one's sweetheart, one must first come retrieve her from the neighbor's, it appears."

Blinking up at him, a smile suddenly lit her features. "I believe so."

She turned to one of the Tarleton's slaves. "Could you retrieve my pelisse, please?"

Mr. Tarleton's large features puckered in distaste. "I'll leave you two to your own devices. I have guests to entertain. Good day."

Phillip moved to her side, took Martha's hand, and raised it to his lips. When he looked up, satisfaction flowed through him at the pink that stained her cheeks. Miss Osborne did share his affection. "We have some appointments to keep, my love."

She raised her eyebrows. Soon the coat was brought and Phillip assisted her into it. He lifted tendrils of silky red curls from her neck, wishing he could press kisses there. But he indeed did have errands. Within one hour he was to meet with his contact, the garrison commander, who was riding in from Charles City to report to the committee about James River traffic and concerns.

He had to speak with Martha about what her friends were up to by having British naval officers at their home. Once outside, he assisted her up into the carriage and draped a heavy blanket across her lap.

"Where are we going?"

He got in beside her and took the reins. "The Nesting Heron."

"That den of iniquity?" The disreputable tavern sat at the northwest outskirts of Williamsburg. She licked her dry lips. "You jest?"

"Not at all."

"Why would you take me there?" First he shows up after no word and now what?

He grinned at her as he directed the horses to turn onto the road to Charles City. "Perhaps I'm going to hand you over to pirates."

"I think you mean those watermen who claim they were privateers but are no better than pirates." She clasped her hands together wishing she could wring an apology out of Phillip for failing to contact her. He'd gotten her hopes up and then left her waiting.

"Either way. But it seems that since you were having a rendezvous with the British navy, perhaps those fine officers will rescue you."

"Not I! The Tarletons are playing a dangerous game inviting those men into their home." Her fingernails bit into her palms. "And you engage in a risky match with me if you believe you can show up with no explanation..."

Phillip directed the horses to pass another carriage on the road. "I take it you didn't receive my message."

"No."

"Ah. My apologies."

They passed the glossy burgundy brougham and Phillip passed the reins into one hand. He

113

covered hers with the other. "One of my uncle's men was to get word to you."

A weight seemed to lift from her heart.

They rode on discussing what they knew of the Tarletons and the relationship between Christopher and Graham. It was hard for Martha to concentrate, being so close to Phillip and inhaling the spicy scent of his cologne.

"I confess I don't know exactly why the militia wants a meeting with me, but I know I must see them. I conjecture they may want more horses."

"And since you were in Williamsburg you decided to drag me along?"

He nodded.

"How very romantic." She laughed. Thankfully, the drizzle had stopped and the sun emerged from the clouds.

In a short while, they entered The Nesting Heron. Not to raucous music, as she'd expected, but to a trio of men playing fiddle in the front right corner. One, a man with a long salt-and-pepper queue, kept time with a shoe whose stitching had failed, revealing a dark stocking beneath.

Instead of the buxom serving wenches she'd imagined, there were several male servers. With red scarves tied around their necks and white caps atop their heads, the burly men carried trays of steaming potted pies on massive trays held high overhead. Phillip grasped her arm and tugged her forward, weaving through the mass of watermen. The scent of brackish water, mingled with sweat and fish odors, tempted Martha to pull her handkerchief from her reticule and press it to her nose.

A waterman eyed her, then Phillip, before tipping his cocked hat and returning to his ale.

Two uniformed militiamen occupied seats at the far wall by a window, curtains drawn closed. Neither rose when she and Phillip approached.

"A woman! You've brought a lady with you?" The man with a scar across his brow frowned but stood.

The dark-haired officer with him rose, smiled at Martha, and made a brief bow. "I'm Major Danner and this is Sergeant Williams. Please have a seat."

She looked to Phillip.

He waved toward the seat that Sergeant Williams was adjusting for her. Was it her imagination or did the militiaman position the chair farther away from himself?

Phillip turned to look at her as he settled into his own chair.

The major waved a passing servant over. "Smuggler's Feast for my friends. And be sure to put it on his account." He laughed.

Phillip chuckled, too.

The men exchanged pleasantries and then briskly engaged in a hushed conversation about horseflesh. Martha tuned in and out as Phillip negotiated prices on sales to the army. She glanced around the room. As time went on, no one was seated at the tables that formed a half circle around them. When a small group of newcomers arrived and headed toward them, fully a dozen watermen stood and formed a wall between themselves and the militia.

"What hey!" a man's deep voice bellowed.

The major, Phillip, and the sergeant continued to chat as though nothing had happened. She patted Phillip's arm. "There's a fracas."

All three men casually reached into their coat pockets, drew forth weapons, and laid them on the table.

"Got it, Tommy?" Sergeant Williams called out as he stood and narrowed his eyes at the crowd.

A slender man, who'd been behind the oak bar, yelled back, "It's just Carter Williams, again claiming he's your cousin, Sergeant!"

The man groaned and his cheeks flushed. "Let him on then, men!"

The crowd parted and a young, dark-haired man, attired in country gentry clothing, strolled back toward them, adjusting the lapels of his tailored great coat.

"Carter Williams," she whispered as a million memories flooded her mind. Her mother taking her to Shirley Plantation for fox hunting events. Her mother playing with the dogs. Her mother bringing her on her very first hunt with the Queen Anne Hunt Club.

"Martha." Mischief glinted in his eyes.

Tears pooled in her eyes as Martha looked up. "It's been so long, I feared you'd forgotten who I was."

Carter bent and kissed her hand. "I should no more forget so beautiful a flower as Martha Osborne as I should my own image in the mirror."

Heat warmed her neck and she pressed her free hand there to cover her embarrassment. Of all the young Tidewater men she'd met over the years, here was one who had never, not once, despised her because of her parents. "Carter..." She couldn't manage any other words.

Phillip stood and grasped her elbow. "Are you two friends?"

Carter was many years her junior. Although they traveled in some of the same social circles, those had diminished since her mother's death.

Once more, Carter raised her bare hand to his lips and pressed a firm, lingering kiss there. "Indeed, I know Martha well. She and I used to bay at the hounds. Do you remember that, Speedy?"

"Speedy?" Phillip thrust his chin upward.

"So-called for her speed in the hunt."

She laughed. "Don't call me that dreadful nickname, or I shall dump a bowl of water on your head like I did your brother."

"A highlight of the social season, I assure you!" He straightened, adjusted his ascot tie, and sighed. "I have missed you, Martha. Wish that old she-dragon still let you out for the hunts."

The two officers had also risen and now cleared their throats.

"I'm not here to see you, my dear, but rather my faux cousin."

"That's rich!" Sergeant Williams assisted Martha back into her seat and leaned in. "He's no more my cousin than he is your twin sister, Miss Osborne."

If only Martha could pass for Christopher's twin brother for the race. She looked up into the sergeant's twinkling dark eyes. "I assure you he is not!"

"Indeed!" Carter grabbed another Windsor chair and pulled it up between her and the sergeant, so close that his knee pressed through her skirts and bumped her leg. Startled, she jerked in Phillip's direction at the same time that he wrapped an arm possessively around her back. Eyes widening, she turned to face him and instead of focusing on his handsome features, she was struck by the jealousy burning in his eyes.

She averted her gaze, uneasy, but couldn't help from smiling. He cared enough for her that he wished to stake his claim. *Good. Let him.*

Carter poured himself some ale from the jug atop the table. "You still race down to Russell Plantation, Martha? To Scotch Tom's Woods?"

Her stomach clenched. She'd forgotten how Carter, like her brother, knew her secrets. "Do you think I would? A gentlewoman such as myself?"

Martha hoped and prayed he did not. For if he did, might he have divulged that information to someone else?

Chapter 9

Beneath him, Othello shifted uneasily, as though sensing Phillip's mission. If Carter Williams, who proved a fount of knowledge about water traffic and potential support for the militia, was correct then this was Martha's favorite haunt on the peninsula. When the two officers escorted Martha out to their curricle, Williams privately shared more about her skill as a horsewoman. Still, was this upcoming race safe for her? Phillip would test the landscape himself in Scotch Tom's Woods. How ironic that his beloved had ridden for years across his great-uncle's property.

Movement from the tree line caught his eye. Someone lurked just beyond the old Indian path that bordered the river. Casually, Phillip maneuvered his reins into one hand and felt for his pistol. The horseman emerged into the sunlight, Tarleton's sorrel easily recognizable.

Was Phillip yet being played the fool? Surely Martha wasn't using the race as a ruse to meet with Tarleton? He'd much rather she'd resumed her friendship with Carter Williams than was anywhere near this cad. His cousin Miranda had been taken in by the rogue's charms, and look what had happened to her. He clenched his teeth, a muscle in his jaw pulsing. He'd promised himself he'd never be jealous of anyone again after the strain George's marriage had placed on their relationship.

Tarleton mustn't have noticed Phillip, for he returned to the secrecy of the woods as Galileo cantered into the sunlit clearing. Martha's hair streamed behind her, and his heart caught in his chest. She was so beautiful, so intelligent, so wrong for Tarleton or Williams. Her form was perfection, her mount exceptional. Here was the one person in all of Tidewater, Virginia who could actually challenge him.

As she neared the woods, Tarleton didn't come forth as Phillip expected. But then suddenly, his sorrel shot out and Martha's mare reared up. Phillip kicked his feet into Othello's side. He bent low as the horse moved from a quick walk, to a trot, and then a full out gallop. Martha remained seated as Tarleton grabbed her reins. *Miscreant.* Scaring both her and her mare could have had grave consequences. But by the time he neared them, Martha, face pale, had calmed her mount.

Tarleton whirled his horse around to face Phillip. "What are you doing here?"

"I could ask you the same."

"I'm free to ride where I wish." Tarleton directed his sorrel to face Martha. "What are you doing in these woods by yourself?"

"I've been exercising my brother's horse for him." Martha glanced quickly at Tarleton and then at him, her eyes begging him to do something.

Tarleton gave a curt laugh. "I doubt seriously that he requires your assistance."

This could not have been a planned meeting. And if not, then what was this? First, though, Phillip had to protect Martha and her reputation.

The younger man began to encircle Martha. "You should be more careful being out in these woods by yourself. You never know who might be here."

"Mr. Tarleton, if you are trying to pretend that Miss Osborne wasn't riding out here to meet with you, then you are doing a poor job of convincing me." Phillip forced his face into a placid expression. Clearly, such was not Tarleton's intention at all, but Phillip needed to find out what his game was.

"Why would I do that? My mother has given us permission to court and has encouraged it. We have no need for secrecy."

From the corner of his eye, Martha's shocked expression revealed a different truth.

Phillip urged his gelding to move between Martha and the young cad, who'd finally brought the red horse to a halt. He cleared his throat. "In fact, Martha and I have an agreement. We do have need for privacy. And if you tell anyone that I rode out here to meet with her…"

Martha raised her chin. "Phillip has already averted a duel with my brother once. I don't want to chance another challenge from him."

"You two?" Tarleton made a disgusted face. "So my father spoke the truth. I didn't believe it."

"It's true." Narrowing his eyes, Phillip squeezed his knees, urging Othello to move closer.

"I'll keep your secret." Tarleton lifted his hat and then returned it to his head.

When the sorrel cantered off Martha drew in a deep breath, and then exhaled loudly. "First of all, our understanding is…."

From the scowl on Phillip's face, she'd obviously angered him. "Martha, please tell me you had not planned on meeting Tarleton?"

"No. Not at all." She patted Galileo's head and avoided looking into Phillip's eyes. What must he think of her?

"What were you doing out here by yourself?"

"I can take care of myself." She stared at him. Instead of an arrogant male attitude, his eyes appeared kind, his mouth downturned slightly. *He's disappointed in me.*

"I have no doubt you believe you can. And you've obviously earned the nickname Williams gave you."

Phillip drew in closer until his leg brushed against her riding habit and she gasped. "I've had no trouble until today."

"I always bring a friend with me when I ride alone." He patted a bulge in his coat pocket. "I'd suggest you ask your brother to accompany you next time."

She hung her head as heat singed her cheeks. "This is his horse. My stepmother sold mine."

"I'll get you another." The warmth in his voice coursed through her like honeyed tea.

Raising her chin, eyes widening, she saw that his offer seemed sincere.

"I am all sincerity, Martha. My affianced must have her own mount for when we ride." He winked at her.

Martha's heartbeat ratcheted up in excitement. She couldn't help but tease him. "If that is your idea of a proposal, sir, it leaves much to be desired."

A cloud passed over his features, darkening them. "Perhaps you will reconsider later."

She tensed and Galileo pawed at the ground. "Oh Phillip…"

He pierced her with his gaze. "If you hadn't planned on meeting Tarleton, then why was he here?"

"I don't know."

Phillip surveyed the area. Heavily wooded at the edges, the open meadow was traversed by a well-ridden horse path.

"We'll have to pray he was only here to spy on those looking for a short cut for the race."

There were better places to divert and gain an advantage. "Don't forget your promise if I win." Which she would. She had to. If only she could trust Phillip to get Johnny home for her. But with him showing up in these woods, was he spying on her? And was his finding her at the Tarletons' home a ruse? Why had he taken her with him to meet those men at The Nesting Heron?

"I haven't forgotten. And I believe Johnny would be best left where he is."

It felt like a cold dipper of York River water had been poured down her back. "We'll see about that." Martha turned her mount back to face home, and they cantered off toward Williamsburg, soon leaving Phillip in their dust.

Remorse rode with her. For if Phillip did have her best interests at heart, might he be correct? Would Johnny be safer away from home?

Chapter 10

Phillip hadn't replied to Martha's note nor had he sent any missives in a fortnight. Heart broken, Martha donned Christopher's clothing. The day of the race arrived and with it the foreboding that winning this race wasn't worth losing him. Perhaps she already had. In the privacy of her bedchamber she'd dressed before dawn.

With each bit of masculine attire added, Martha's soul weighed down further. What if something should happen to her? What of Johnny? With her brother, Christopher, so ill, how could she be sure he'd be there to help with their younger sibling?

She slipped out to the stables, inhaling the sweet scent of fresh hay.

"Are you ready?" Their groomsman assisted her up onto the horse. She raised her leg over the saddle, suddenly self-conscious.

"I'll have to be." Foolish, headstrong girl — wasn't that what Letitia called her? How could Martha have been so imprudent as to enter this race?

Soon, she and Galileo arrived at Bruton. All the young men, astride their horses, circled the courtyard, warming up their horses for the race. Her brother wasn't on close terms with many of the young men in the race, so it wasn't difficult to avoid them. She kept her chin tucked down and avoided eye contact.

The horses, sensing the importance of the event and the nervous energy of their riders, nickered to one another. A tall figure strode toward the cluster. Dr. Shield? What was he doing here? Was Phillip here? She'd not looked for him and had sent him a note to pay her no heed at the race lest he reveal her secret.

The surgeon, dressed in a tailored greatcoat and buff breeches, held a pistol in his right hand. He waved it overhead, gaining everyone's attention. Seeing the young men pulling their mounts into a line, Martha followed suit but remained slightly back and away from them.

In less than a minute, a shot was fired and off horses and riders flew, down the streets of Williamsburg. Once they left the village for the countryside, Martha squeezed her knees and bent low over Galileo's broad back. With much concentration, they shot past rider after rider. She saw an opening between the two front riders, Graham with his sorrel and a lean young rider, one of her friend's brothers. She blinked in appreciation for the boy's skill, which she'd not known until that moment. But she and Galileo maneuvered between the two front runners and galloped on through the clearing.

Once the field opened wide, Martha gave Galileo his head. Up ahead was the secret shortcut behind Pratt's Plantation. Martha was far enough in the lead that she could divert without anyone seeing her. She kicked Galileo's side and laid herself out almost flat on him as they flew over the field and then rerouted through the trees on the old Indian path.

Her heart hammered as they cantered into the woods. The tree canopy crowded together overhead, blocking out much of the sun. They slowed. Birdsong called out over Galileo's hoof beats and the sound of Martha's heart in her ears. She adjusted the reins as well as her seat and legs as they entered an uneven stretch of path on a curve.

They'd rounded a corner when suddenly something fell from overhead. Martha looked up as heavy, dank-smelling netting fell over her, darkening her world. Martha struggled to keep Galileo upright as he screamed out a neigh of protest.

Down they went into a low pit as she was slung against his massive head. The horse neighed in pain. Had his leg been broken? *Oh God, dear Lord help me.*

Martha struggled to remove the damp cording that had dropped onto them, finally pulling it free as Galileo abruptly slumped down. She pushed off of his side before he could crush her leg, heart hammering. Her breath came in short bursts as she knelt on the horse's side. She patted his head. "Poor dear."

Suddenly another horse cantered into the woods then came to a halt nearby. "Tut tut! Bad bit of luck, old girl." Graham's taunt was followed by an eerie laugh.

How could he do this?

"Couldn't accept my family's bone of offering could you?" He drew closer and peered down his patrician nose from atop his horse.

"What?" She shook in both rage and fear.

"You could have married me and all would have been well."

He was insane. "Graham, you know you don't love me!"

"What does love have to do with it? Your father has his head too far into his books to care about his wife and her activities, but you and your brother — well, we tried, but don't seem to have contained you."

Her back ached and she tried to stand. "Help me out. I don't know what you mean." But she feared she might. "If you don't want to be my husband, why marry me?"

"To keep your nose out of our plans."

"What plans?" So it was exactly as Phillip feared. The Tarletons were colluding with the English navy, providing them information. That's why Graham had befriended Christopher, a talented mapmaker, in the first place.

He laughed. "Your brother should have stopped snooping around my maps and he'd be fine, too. Too bad you two don't know what's for your own good."

"You're making no sense." Could she convince him she knew nothing?

"I'll have to deal with Christopher, too."

She shivered at the evil in his voice but Martha had to stay strong. "Just get me out of here and help me with the horse."

"Oh, I shall help." He reached into his pocket and lazily began pouring powder into his pistol, light filtering through the woods to illuminate its silvery shaft. "Too bad my horse will have spooked when I put your horse down."

"No!" Martha patted Galileo's head, her hand shaking.

"A shame I'll miss him and shoot you. All's fair in love and war and all that nonsense, you know..."

"What?" She gasped and slumped back down, her brother's horse's breaths coming more slowly now even as hers increased.

So this was to be it? Dear God, help Johnny. *Help them know the truth, Lord. And protect our country from Graham and other men like him who would return our free land to the British. And Lord, please protect Phillip's heart.*

A large, heavily-muscled, black gelding cantered into the woods, spitting dirt behind its hooves. *Thank God. Phillip on Othello.* Graham's horse reared, his gun falling to the ground as he was thrown. His horse came down on his chest and Graham cried out in pain.

What Phillip had just witnessed shredded years from his life. The woman he loved, in a pit with her brother's horse shuddering beneath her. *Tarleton standing over her loading a gun.*

After dismounting, he tied the horse off and retrieved his pistol, lest Tarleton was feigning injury. The sorrel trotted off. Did his owner lay dying? Phillip ran first to Martha and pulled her up into his arms. Her hair fell from beneath her cap.

"Are you all right?"

"No." Tears streamed down her face. "I don't know."

He pressed Martha close to him and kissed the top of her head. Curls freed from where pins had come loose. "Thank God he didn't…"

Martha pulled away and glanced toward Tarleton. Phillip took in the odd angle of the man's neck and knew he'd not survived. Martha shuddered out a sigh and began to weep.

Patting her back, Phillip's concerns of war boiled down to one individual he most wanted to protect forever—the woman he now held in his arms.

"You frightened me half to death. Don't ever do that again!" He held her close against his beating heart as he whispered into her ear, "I love you, Martha."

She pulled free and looked up at him. Slowly, he lowered his head, but she grasped his neck and pulled him closer, her tears wetting his cheeks as they deepened the kiss. She smelled of sunshine and verdant fields, her hair of faint rosewater and the salt of perspiration. Her lips tasted of the sweetest tea and finest Demerara sugar. Her curves, obviously restrained and bound, were nonetheless obvious to him as he clutched her closer. Oh sweet heavens, she must become his wife. He pulled back and tucked her head beneath his chin, rubbing her back as his heart tried to pound its way out of his chest. He must restrain himself. And although Tarleton had been a wicked man, his death must be reported.

"I'm taking you home," Phillip whispered into her ear as he lifted Martha up beside him on Othello.

They'd almost reached his home when she collapsed, slumping into him.

Chapter 11

Phillip paced the corridor outside Martha's sick room, where Dr. Shield examined her.

Maman's dusky rose perfume accompanied her as she took his arm. "Go sit."

"I feel better standing." Not that anything made him feel better.

"Stephen will take good care of your Martha."

His Martha. He loved the sound of it. But had he compromised her health, her very life, by not stopping her from racing with those young men to the steeple?

The French blue-paneled door opened as the surgeon exited the room.

Phillip clenched his fists. "Shall she make a full recovery?"

Maman pressed her fingers to her lips.

"She's suffered some injuries." Stephen crossed his arms. "But I expect a week or two abed will bring recovery."

"Praise God!" His mother uttered the words Phillip couldn't seem to manage.

He sank onto the chair. "Thank you." *Thank you, God.*

His friend nodded. "I'm going to get her brother and bring him to you."

Phillip raised his head. "Is it true then? Has her father gone?"

132

"Yes, but let's not discuss that here."

"Later," Phillip mouthed.

Maman took Stephen's hand. "You've had a busy day."

"But with a happy ending, praise God."

"Come let's get some refreshments." She turned to Phillip. "I'll bring you and your fiancée some tea in a bit. We have much to plan."

Looking into her glittering eyes, Phillip knew his mother was already setting into motion a wedding over which he and Martha would have little control. Despite the gravity of the situation, he almost laughed.

After they left, Phillip slipped into the room. Martha had a right to know everything. But was now the time to tell her?

Taking one glance at her wan face, eyes closed shut in sleep, Phillip sank into the padded boudoir chair beside the bed. *Lord, who are we really in Christ? Who did You make us to be? Restore Martha to complete health. Don't let the sins of the father or, in this case, stepmother, be visited any further upon her. Show us your will in our lives—together. In Jesus's name, Amen.*

When he opened his eyes, Martha looked up at him. "Did you know I thought you were my angel?"

"What?" He knelt by the bed and took her hand between his own.

She gave a faint laugh but then closed her eyes in pain. "I prayed for help. And you came to the baker's shop."

"I'm glad God sent me. I had no idea of His plans for me." He pressed a kiss to her hand and heard her soft intake of breath.

"We're to be wed?" Martha's words slurred. Perhaps the physician had given her some laudanum.

"If you'll have me."

"I heard your mother…" Her words trailed off and her eyes closed again.

He rose and sat back in the uncomfortable chair, still holding her hand.

The door creaked open and Father eased in, holding a silver tray with two cups and saucers and a teapot. He set them down on a tea table in front of the window and poured into one of Mother's blue and white Limoges china teacups, reserved for special occasions.

"Have you told her, Son?" Father passed the cup of steaming gunpowder tea to Phillip.

He took the tea. "If you mean about Letitia, no, nor really about the rest."

Huffing out a sigh, Father lowered himself into a straight back chair by the table. "I'm afraid there is more."

"I think she's asleep. Do you want to tell me?"

"Best done before the boy arrives. You see, his mother is believed dead."

"Letitia?" He'd heard she was reported missing. That American spies in England could no longer track her. "Dead?"

"Yes. We have it on good authority that she and her daughter departed from her parents' estate in Kent and traveled to her lover's estate in Devon, yet she never arrived."

Phillip's head began to pound. "Poor Johnny."

"Yes." Father poured himself some tea in the cup intended for Martha. "'Tis better than witnessing his mother hung for being a spy, don't you think?"

So Letitia was indeed a British spy. "And the lad?"

"As we believed. Osborne is not his father."

"Yet Stephen said Professor Osborne has left for England."

"Some men think with their hearts rather than their heads."

"Or have neither." Phillip shouldn't speak with such scorn of his future father-in-law, but what in the world was the man doing?

"If my beautiful wife and my daughter were missing, I'd want to know what happened." Father gazed at Martha in paternal admiration. "Yet, unbeknownst to him, he almost lost another daughter."

Both Phillip and his father exhaled a sigh. "It will be hard keeping Martha at rest."

"Especially once her brother arrives at the house."

"The admiral will never lay hands on Johnny to claim him," Phillip ground out. "He may have fathered him, but…"

Father's shocked expression bespoke his agreement.

"And Professor Osborne…"

"Don't blame the professor too much. I've heard his in-laws, despite their lofty aristocratic status, sent a lengthy missive demanding that he come help find their daughter and granddaughter."

"Is that so?"

"Young Osborne and his elder brother will both benefit from your counsel, Phillip."

"Christopher is now on his own."

"At least Dr. Shield assures us that Christopher's illness is a malady brought on by anxiety and not a disease."

"Now that this race has ended and his maps have been recovered…"

"And Tarleton dead."

"What a sad waste."

The bed creaked as Martha raised her head from the pillow. Her eyelids briefly fluttered and then her head fell back. Phillip rose and pressed a hand to her brow, then felt for a heartbeat. Thankfully, it thrummed strong beneath his fingers.

"Let's take this conversation downstairs, Father."

"I'll send your mother in to sit with her."

The bedchamber door opened, revealing Maman.

"You men, shoo!" Maman fluttered her hands at them as though they were pigeons come too close to the house and disturbing the yellow finches she so loved to feed.

"Going." Father planted a brusque kiss on her cheek.

She offered the other cheek to Phillip to kiss as he passed by. If he had a marriage half as good as his parents' had been, he'd be a blessed man.

Martha awoke with a crushing headache and pain in her sides, which were tightly wrapped with cotton strips. The pungent odor of liniment permeated the air. Beneath her, the mattress was firm rather than soft as her bed was at home. When she opened her eyes, there was Johnny, playing with toy soldiers on a window bench seat.

"Johnny?" Her voice sounded breathless.

"Marty!" He ran toward the bed but then skidded to a halt. "Mr. Phillip said not to hug you. But I can give you a kiss, can't I?"

Tears pooled in her eyes as her little brother pressed a feather-light kiss to her cheek.

A dark-skinned young woman came into the room, her bright coral headwrap accentuating the colors in her unusual gown of striped cotton. This was no slave. "I'm here to help you get up and take care of your needs." She cast a glance at Johnny.

Martha understood. "Yes. Thank you." She needed to be cleaned up.

But her brother didn't move.

"Johnny, do you know where to find Mr. Phillip?"

"Um hum." He glanced between her and the servant.

"We gonna get your sister ready, in case she wanta get up and wander these big hallways upstairs and see all the pretty pictures we have."

The woman bent, placing her hands above her knees, her voice soothing.

Martha eased up onto her elbows. "Run down to see Mr. Phillip, then, all right?"

"All right."

"Your brother Christopher will be arriving soon."

"Huzzah!" Johnny ran out.

When the door slammed behind him, Martha flinched.

The servant sighed and latched the door. "For privacy, Missy. Now, you let me help you."

"Thank you."

"Your horse is fine. My man tells me your Galileo gonna run again one day."

Tears streamed down Martha's cheeks.

The woman sat beside her on the bed and began to brush out Martha's hair. "You and Johnny gonna love livin' here, Missy. Don't you worry any."

She'd not left this bedroom, but Martha had heard stories of the grand estate.

Setting the brush down, the servant revealed her even white teeth. "Master Phillip is a good man. You're a lucky woman."

"I'm blessed."

"Not my place to say, but Master George's wife, she make a big mistake when she pass up Mr. Phillip. Now look what happenin'."

"What do you mean?"

"Mr. Phillip gonna have this big ol' place, not Mr. George."

Father poured himself a crystal snifter of brandy. "Now that you are marrying, your mother and I wish to make a few things clear to you."

Phillip turned from the bank of mullioned windows overlooking the glittering water of the York River. "Such as?"

"This home and half the acreage will be yours."

"Not George's?" And Andrée's?

Father's silver head bobbed. "George has already received his inheritance—that of the land, the academy, and his home."

"And he understands this?" Phillip didn't need his brother despising him over worldly goods.

"Yes." Father's clipped word brooked no room for an argument.

"Thank you. I don't know what to say."

"The horses on the farm are all owned by you anyway, Son. They bring a great deal of income to the maintaining of this property."

Phillip ducked his chin. He'd never complained about helping. He did, after all, use the stables and the land, as well as dwelt in the house. And these were his parents. "I didn't expect you to leave me the plantation, though."

"With the militia making their headquarters here soon, who knows what the place will look like in a few years."

They both gave a curt laugh. "But we'd be protected."

Phillip squinted to look out the window and count the masts on the vessel approaching the wharf. "I wonder how much information Tarleton fed to the Admiralty."

"Young Osborne didn't realize his so-called friend was giving British naval intelligence his maps with detailed information about the rivers and waterways. He won't face any reprimands from the Commonwealth, especially since there is no war."

"Not yet." Phillip swallowed back the bile that rose in his throat.

The schooner approached the wharf and their men rushed to secure the vessel. Christopher Osborne had been betrayed by his former best friend, now dead. His stepmother and half-sister were missing. And his father had left the college for England.

At least Martha had Phillip and his family. They'd offer the same to her brothers. Phillip straightened his jacket and strode out to greet his future brother-in-law.

He'd let go of his past. Andrée wasn't the woman God had planned for him. Martha and her brothers would be under his protection now—right where they were meant to be. And despite the extra *burden* suddenly Phillip's soul felt lighter than ever. He was free to claim a new life. Who knew where God would take them all?

Epilogue

"Virginia in spring is a fine sight indeed." Mrs. Paulson pressed a bouquet of forsythia, dogwood blossoms, and early roses into Martha's hands. "But not nearly as beautiful as the bride before me."

Martha blinked back tears. "Thank you."

Someone knocked on the door. "It's time," Christopher called out.

"I'll be praying for you." Her almost mother-in-law patted Martha's shoulder.

"With only the finest of Virginia waiting on the lawn and a contingent of militia, too, what have I to be nervous of?" Martha would keep her wits about her only by God's provision.

Christopher stepped aside to allow Mrs. Paulson to depart. He turned to Martha. "Don't forget the boys from the academy."

"How could I?"

Christopher whistled. "I already threatened to tie the younger ones to a tree if they don't stop climbing them."

"Oh my. Not Johnny?"

"No, he's carrying around a basket of flower petals with the Lightfoots' youngest girl."

"Throwing them on the other children, I imagine?"

"Exactly."

They laughed and her anxiety lifted. "I'm going to be married, Christopher, can you believe it?"

He sighed. "I can believe that. What I can't believe is our stepmother went to such lengths to avenge her father's death."

Martha's chest tightened. "Killed in the American Revolution, right here in Virginia."

"And her aristocratic mother left impoverished until she'd remarried the duke."

"Letitia wasted her life."

"If she's dead."

Shuddering, Martha smoothed her wedding dress. "At least Emily has been found. We have that to be thankful for."

"Father wrote that Emily believes her mother is biding her time with the Admiral."

Johnny wasn't their sibling and neither was Emily, if reports were true. Still, they loved both. "Will she return with Father?"

Features tightening in regret, Christopher ignored her question and extended his arm. "We best be going."

"Christopher?"

"Yes?"

"Would you really have dueled Phillip?"

"I was too busy trying to figure out what Graham was up to. I knew he must despise me to pursue Miranda. Before that, I wondered at his intense interest in my maps for my cartography classes. But afterward…" He bit out a retort.

"Let's not think of that now. I'm sorry I brought it up." Goodness, these wedding nerves had her chattering like a schoolgirl. "You'll soon be married, too, brother, won't that be fine?"

"And father to Graham's child." Although his voice held tension, there was no resentment in his words.

"To Miranda's child and my niece twice over once you marry," Martha enthused.

He laughed. "Yes, there's that."

"Will you love her?"

"Of course I will."

"And not do as Father has?"

"Never." He tugged her arm. "Now come, let's get this thing done."

Standing before the preacher, surrounded by hundreds of onlookers, Martha's knees shook so badly that she feared she'd sink into the green lawn. As though sensing her distress, Phillip moved closer and took her elbow, sending a sensation of warmth and support through her. All would be well.

Somehow their vows had been said because the preacher was looking at Martha and Phillip expectantly. She'd been aware that she'd repeated some words, but for the life of her couldn't recall for certain what she'd said. All she recalled was staring up into the handsome face of the angel who would be her husband. A lock of golden hair fell across his forehead as he bent and pressed a gentle kiss to her lips. The look in his eyes sent a shiver of anticipation through her. She was Phillip's wife. Mrs. Paulson. This was her home, her family. Tremors began in her neck and traveled down to her satin slippered feet. Phillip pulled her close to his side as they wheeled around to face the onlookers.

"I give you Mr. and Mrs. Paulson. What therefore God hath joined together, let not man put asunder."

The crowd erupted in "Huzzahs!" from the militia, claps of approval from the gentry, and from the corner of her eye Martha spied baskets of flower petals tossed onto the heads of the children, some of whom now wrestled on the ground. Johnny raced down the aisle between the chairs, straight at them. Christopher rose to intervene but her little brother shot past him and right at them. He launched himself into their arms.

Phillip winked at her before hoisting Johnny up onto his shoulders. Linking her arm through her husband's, the three stepped forward—ready to face whatever lay ahead—with God's help.

The End

Thank you for reading *The Steeplechase*! If you enjoyed it, would you please consider posting a review?

Acknowledgements

Thanking God for the ability to keep writing! My family is owed a debt of gratitude for their support. Thank you, Regina Fujitani, who served as professional Beta reader. Blessings to my Beta readers: Chris Granville, Caryl Kane, Tina Rice, and Gracie Yost.

Advance readers – Sydney Anderson, Sonja Hoeke Nishimoto, Britney Adams, Joy Gibson, Kay Moorhouse, Teresa Danner Kander, Bonnie Roof, Deanna Stevens, Betti Mace, "Chappy" Debbie Mitchell, Nancy McLeroy, Amy Campbell, and Emily Yost.

Thank you to cover designer and publisher Cynthia Hickey for putting together this collection. God bless my friend and editor Narielle Living.

I'd also like to acknowledge my Pagels' Pals reader group members – thanks for being there for me! And my Overcoming with God Overcoming with God blog "Angels" for their ongoing support – Diana Flowers, Teresa Matthews, Noela Nancarrow, and Bonnie Roof. I'd also like to thank the bloggers at Colonial Quills and members of our Colonial American Christian Writers group.

Much thanks to my friend Christy Hudgins Zumbrun, a lifetime resident of Hampton Roads, for brainstorming with me about our waterways into Williamsburg! That was helpful.

Thank you, Martha Jane Osborn Phillips and Rev. Dr. Paul Lucien Phillips for letting me "borrow" your names and play with them a little. Rev. and Mrs. Phillips have had cameo roles in my other stories but this is their debut as hero and heroine! Martha and Phillip were a wonderful couple to hang out with, like their real-life counterparts!

Equestrian Glenye Oakford has been such a support and encouragement and has been so helpful with my horse questions. And I want to thank Misty White NP and Dr. Mark Croucher – you two keep me moving so I can continue writing books!

I'm glad God put all of you in my life. I'm blessed.

Editorial Notes

I pray that history buffs, especially those who love horses, will give me an allowance on the time frame for my novella. The Steeplechase itself was not begun, as a sport, until later in the 1800s, well after this 1810 time frame. What I envisioned as a "What if?" was young gentlemen of the Tidewater area preparing for the possibility of war, again, with England. Since I live in this area now, I thought—"what if" I lived here or had children, including adult children, and I sensed the build-up to another confrontation with the British. In fact, the War of 1812 is considered by some to be the second war of independence.

More "What ifs" were—what if you were an Anglican priest (we have beautiful old Anglican churches in the Commonwealth of Virginia that sat empty during this time) and you had no flock? What happened to you if you were an American and had no desire to go to England? When the very notion of using a Book of Common Prayer, intended for British citizens, would label you as anti-American? And what of your children? Hence this story was born.

Privateers were indeed enlisted to help combat the British during the War of 1812. Young men living along the coast of young America were abducted and forced to serve aboard British ships. Transportation around the peninsula of Virginia would have been by boat, horseback, carriage, or a combination of all. As my husband pointed out – "They had no motorboats back then!"

"Light Horse Harry" Lee, or Henry Lee III, Revolutionary War hero, Governor of Virginia, and father to Robert E. Lee had a difficult life. As indicated in the story, he spent time in a debtor's prison and wrote a book that helped in covering some of those obligations. His children with Anne Carter Lee resided at Shirley Plantation during that time, in Charles City. The plantation is open to visitors and offers tours. You can even see Robert E. Lee's child's bed in the Great House.

Wanting to visit Bruton Parish and Grace Episcopal Church? Would you be surprised that these colonial era churches, included in this story, are active parishes today? If you visit Colonial Williamsburg, you'll find Bruton at the edge of one corner of the Palace Green. Grace Episcopal is situated on hilltop in historic Yorktown, near the center of old York Towne.

Footnotes:

Song: I Leave My Heart With Thee, (circa 1804-1806), words anonymous, set to music by Mr. James Hook (1746-1827).

Author Biography

Carrie Fancett Pagels "Hearts Overcoming Through Time" is an award-winning and Amazon best-selling Christian historical fiction author. Carrie enjoys reading, traveling, baking, and beading—but not all at the same time! Possessed with an overactive imagination, she loves sharing her stories with others. A psychologist for twenty-five years, she no longer practices. Married for twenty-eight years to the man of her dreams, with a teenage son at home and an adult daughter nearby. Carrie resides in Virginia's Historic Triangle, which is perfect for her fascination with history.

Visit Carrie's blogs: Overcoming with God and Colonial Quills
Website is www.CarrieFancettPagels.com
Carrie has an author page on Facebook (where you can sign up for her monthly newsletter), is on Twitter (cfpagels), goodreads, Pinterest, LinkedIn, and Google+.

Other books/stories by Carrie Fancett Pagels:

Saving the Marquise's Granddaughter (White Rose/Pelican, June 2016).

9 Historical Women Win More than a Blue Ribbon at the Fair

THE
Blue Ribbon
BRIDES
COLLECTION

Cynthia Hickey, Gina Welborn
Jennifer AlLee, Angela Breidenbach, Darlene Franklin,
Carrie Fancett Pagels, Amber Stockton,
Niki Turner, Becca Whitham

Releasing from Barbour Publishing, November, 2016. Includes Carrie's novella, "Requilted with Love."

Return to Shirley Plantation: A Civil War Romance (Hearts Overcoming Press, January 2016) 2nd edition.)

Christmas Traditions, an eight-in-one collection from Forget Me Not Romances (July 2015), #1 Amazon bestseller in Anthologies. Includes Carrie Fancett Pagels' *The Fruitcake Challenge*, also Volume 1 in The Christy Lumber Camp Series.

The Christy Lumber Camp Series Volumes 2 &3

The Substitute Bride (Hearts Overcoming Press, October, 2015), a novella set in Shepherd Michigan and part of the O' Little Town of Christmas collection.

"Snowed In" published in *A Cup of Christmas Cheer* (Guidepost Books, October, 2013).

Made in the USA
Middletown, DE
08 October 2016